"Do you know the mistletoe legend?"

Bret strained to reach the cluster of mistletoe and detach it from the snowy branch. Suddenly, the cluster came free and tumbled through the tree limbs, raining berries and leaves and snowflakes amidst Dani's shouts of delight.

She stretched her hands upward to catch the cluster, laughing.

Bret sprang to the ground beside her. He said softly, "Do you mean the one about kissing?"

Suddenly, their eyes met. The moment between them was poised and expectant, and either one of them, with a word, a breath, a shifted gaze, could have broken it. But no power on earth could have persuaded Dani to move away from Bret then.

She whispered in a husky voice, "Absolutely."

Their lips touched, as they had done many times before. But right from the first instant, they both knew that this time was different....

ABOUT THE AUTHOR

One of the original authors for the Harlequin
American Romance series, Rebecca Flanders has
written over twenty-five novels. Extraordinarily
versatile, she is a master at creating heroes whom
we all fall in love with—such as the devastatingly
charming Bret Underwood in *Under the
Mistletoe*. Rebecca also currently writes
mainstream contemporary and historical fiction.
She lives in the mountains of Georgia with
her daughter.

Books by Rebecca Flanders

HARLEQUIN AMERICAN ROMANCE

Don't miss any of our special offers. Write to us at the
following address for information on our newest releases.

Harlequin Reader Service
P.O. Box 1397, Buffalo, NY 14240
Canadian address: P.O. Box 603,
Fort Erie, Ont. L2A 5X3

REBECCA FLANDERS

UNDER THE MISTLETOE

Harlequin Books

TORONTO • NEW YORK • LONDON
AMSTERDAM • PARIS • SYDNEY • HAMBURG
STOCKHOLM • ATHENS • TOKYO • MILAN

Published December 1991

ISBN 0-373-16417-3

UNDER THE MISTLETOE

Chapter One

The sound of the mail truck's horn interrupted Bret's fifth lap across the pool. By the time he pulled himself out of the water and dried his face with the towel that was draped across the webbed chair at the pool's edge, the door chimes had already echoed once. Like most California homes—even those as luxurious as his—there wasn't much of a walk from the street to the front door.

He could see the mail carrier's uniform through the glass inset of the front door as he crossed through the kitchen and foyer, leaving wet footprints across the quarry-tile floor. He could also see the registered letter that was the reason his morning swim had been interrupted—a packet of documents from his father's attorney in Clayville that Bret had specifically directed should be sent to his office but that Johnson Webb, with typical small-town stubbornness, had apparently mailed to his home instead.

Towel-drying his hair with one hand, Bret opened the door. "Morning," he said, accepting the pen the carrier offered.

"Just sign right there by the X, if you will."

Bret glanced at the man as he did so. "You're new on this route, aren't you?"

Bret had a natural eye for detail, but it didn't take an experienced detective to realize that this middle-aged, rosy-cheeked man bore no resemblance to the slim, young woman who usually delivered his mail. He was short and round, with a neatly trimmed white beard and a fringe of snowy hair peeking out from his cap from ear to ear and a deep, warm voice that reverberated with more than the usual Southern California friendliness. He looked like a man who enjoyed his job and he made Bret want to smile even through his annoyance at having to interrupt his morning routine to sign for the package.

The letter carrier's blue eyes twinkled as though with some private joke as he replied, "Just filling in during the holidays."

Bret grimaced a little as he glanced across the street at the houses of his neighbors, many of whom had already started decorating their doors with tacky foil wreaths and paper Santas. "Yeah, I guess it is that time again, isn't it? Seems to start earlier and earlier every year."

"Never too early for me," the mailman replied cheerfully, and handed him the package, plus several other envelopes. "Here's the rest of your mail. Have a good day now."

Bret had never heard of a mailman who actually looked forward to Christmas, and he grinned a little as he turned away from the door, glancing through the mail. He tossed the package on the foyer table next to his briefcase so he wouldn't forget to take it to the office, but the rest of the mail wasn't worth saving. Fliers, mail-order catalogs, sweepstakes entries, credit-card offers... How had his name gotten on all those mailing lists, anyway?

Then he stopped. There was one envelope that was completely blank—no return address, no postmark, not even an address. "Hey!" he called, going back to the door. But the mail truck was already gone.

He frowned as he closed the door and started toward the kitchen, examining the envelope. It was probably more junk, he thought and he started to throw it away with the rest of the trash. Then common curiosity got the better of him. He tore open the envelope and was startled to see a hand-written message that began "Dear Bret." He skipped down to the signature and his heartbeat actually jumped as he read "Dani."

For a moment, he could do nothing but stare at the page. Then quickly, he snatched up the envelope again, examining it both front and back. Dani! But how... and why...?

"Weird," he muttered. He hooked his ankle around a chair and pulled it out from the kitchen table. He had to sit down to read this.

Dear Bret,
     I'm never going to mail this, and no one but you would understand why I have to write it down. Tonight, you're getting married...

His heart thudded again. Married? He glanced at the top of the letter, but there was no date. Of course, there wouldn't be, she had never intended to mail it. Married...

Ten years ago, Bret Underwood had married Laura Wheeling, a bright, beautiful liberal-arts major with enough ambition for two women and enough charm for five. He had thought she was exactly what he needed, he had thought he was the luckiest man alive. He had thought, young and starry-eyed as he had been, that he loved her.

His eyes went back to the letter, seeing the words but not reading them. Ten years ago, Dani Griffin had sat down to write this letter because that was what they did when they had a secret too big to keep and too important to tell...they wrote it down. Once it was out of their systems, they tore the message up or hid it away and the urge to tell was gone. Except Dani hadn't torn up this letter. What was the secret she had kept from him on his wedding day that was too important to tell?

He made his eyes focus again. His throat felt dry but he did not reach for the cup of coffee that was cooling at his elbow.

Tonight, you're getting married, and I've tried to be happy for you, I really have, but I think you know I don't approve. What you don't know is why, and that's the secret. There's someone who loves you, Bret, more than Laura ever could, and I think if you knew, it might make a difference. And that's exactly why I can't tell you...because you love Laura, not her, and it might make a dif-- ference. I've never kept a secret from you be-

fore, and I hope you understand why I had to
keep this one. But even if you don't, remember
that I'll always be

> Your best friend,
> Dani

He read the letter again, then once more, slowly.
Then he just sat at the table and gazed out the open
French door that led to the pool.

"Dani, Dani," he murmured, dropping his eyes to
the letter once more. "You always did know how to
get a fellow's day off to a helluva start, didn't you?"

He lifted his cup, but the coffee was cold. He poured
the contents into the sink and refilled the cup, leaning
against the open door as he read the letter again. Ten
years ago...

Ten years ago, he had been ready to shake the dust
of Clayville, Indiana, off his feet and conquer the
world. He had a job lined up that paid more than his
father had ever made in his life, he had Los Angeles,
with all its glamour and tinsel, and a wife who had
dedicated herself to helping him get to the top. He
wouldn't have been able to imagine, nor would he have
believed it had he been told, that everyone wasn't as
happy for him as he was for himself.

Of course, he knew Dani hadn't completely ap-
proved of Laura, but that was only natural. Laura was
a stranger, and no girl, in Dani's eyes, would ever be
good enough for him just as no man would ever be
good enough for Dani as far as Bret was concerned.
But she had never given him any indication that she

objected this strongly to his marriage...or if she had, he had ignored her.

A wry smile touched his lips as he lifted the coffee cup. If she had given him this letter ten years ago, it might have saved him a lot of pain...or it might not have made any difference. At any rate, it was too late to start crying over spilled milk now.

If you knew, it might make a difference. He read the line again, frowning. *There's someone who loves you, Bret....*

Who? Who was it who had loved him all those years ago, and who, if he had known about it, might have saved him from making the biggest mistake of his life? Who could it possibly have been?

His mind drifted back into the past, over the girls he had known...hometown girls with sparkling eyes and curly ponytails, sophisticated college girls, voluptuous starlets... A wistful smile crossed his lips then faded with puzzlement. Which one of them could have changed his life? And how could Dani have known about it when he didn't?

Unless...it was Dani herself.

Embarrassed color stung his neck, and the thought was dismissed almost before it was born. Not Dani. To even consider the possibility made him feel conceited and foolish.

He had a collage of pictures inside his head, pictures of Dani and pictures of himself that when strung together, formed a diary of his life. Dani at five, her fists balled and her eyes glittering as she flung herself into a free-for-all to defend him from some real or imagined insult. Himself at nine, doing the same for her. A mountain of peanut-butter sandwiches shared from Flintstone's lunch boxes in between. Dani in her first grown-up party dress, trying to keep him from trampling all over her new pumps as she taught him to dance. And himself, threatening to tear some poor freshman limb from limb because he had gotten fresh with Dani at the Valentine Ball.

It would be ridiculous to say Bret had never thought of Dani sexually. Every teenage boy thought about every teenage girl sexually. He and Dani used to practice kissing so they'd be sure to do it right with their "real" dates, and there had been times when Bret thought he might like to do more than practice. But they'd been kids then, and Dani had certainly never thought of him that way.

Since they were three years old, Dani Griffin had been his sparring partner, his confidante, his tutor, his counselor; sometimes his worst enemy, but always his best friend. When they'd gone away to separate colleges, her twice-weekly letters were the only things that had kept his head on straight. When his marriage broke up, his long-distance phone bill averaged four hundred dollars a month; God only knew what hers had been. When he had gone home for his mother's funeral five years ago, he and Dani had sat up all night and talked, and he hadn't been ashamed to cry on her shoulder. He had never been as close to anyone in the world as he was to Dani Griffin.

And that night, the night before his wedding, she had kissed him. It was a congratulatory kiss, a good-luck kiss, an I'm-going-to-miss-you-and-hope-you'll-be-happy kiss. But for a moment—for one fleeting, dangerous and wildly promising moment—Bret could have sworn that kiss hovered on the edge of something more. And then it was over and Dani was laughing, and he was sure he imagined it. The next day, he got married and Dani waved goodbye to him from the steps of the church.

She had known all along. But she'd never said a word. And what difference did it make now? What difference would it have made then?

Abruptly, he picked up the phone and started to dial Dani's number. He had barely punched out the area code, however, before he hung up again. Just what was he supposed to say to her? "Say, about this letter you wrote me ten years ago and never intended to mail..." And how had it gotten here, anyway? He went back to the table and looked at the envelope. The whole thing was entirely too disturbing for this hour of the morning, and the only thing that was clear was that he couldn't confront her with it via long distance. In fact, the smart thing to do would be to forget about it—just as Dani apparently had for ten years.

But he couldn't forget about it. He put the letter into his briefcase and took it to work with him, and all the way downtown, he kept wondering. Who was she? Who was the girl who had loved him? And what was he supposed to do about it now?

IN BRET'S OPINION, THERE was no place in the world as depressing as Los Angeles at Christmastime. It was bad enough that the temperature was already eighty-three degrees and the smog layer so thick you could cut it with a knife, but why did all the stores have to use that garish, glittery garland in colors like neon pink and lime green? One window display featured Santa in Hawaiian-print swim trunks and a surf board. Another suggested that Santa's helpers were all models with platinum hair and gold-sequined bikinis. And there was nothing quite as gaudy as a tinfoil Christmas tree flashing with oversize gold bulbs.

Almost every Christmas in Clayville had been a white one, and even without the snow, they had always been cold enough to justify Santa's fur-trimmed suit and cherry red cheeks. After his first year at Berkeley, Bret had sworn he would never spend another frost-bitten winter as long as he lived. Funny how much he missed the cold now. And how he couldn't get the picture of Dani, with her nose chapped and red, and snowflakes in her hair, out of his mind.

By the time he arrived at the fifth-floor offices of Underwood Security Agency he thought he had figured out how the letter had gotten to him, at any rate. Obviously, it must be connected with the envelope from Webb and Webb, Attorneys at Law. Maybe it had accidentally gotten mixed up with the other papers inside and had fallen out.... Maybe Dani had intended to send him a letter or some kind of important paper via the lawyers and had mistakenly sent this letter instead.... Maybe she *had* sent it to him ten years ago and it had only now resurfaced among his father's papers.... None of those solutions was completely acceptable of course, and each of them left a great deal more unanswered than not, but at least they were a start.

Generally, he felt a surge of perfectly justifiable pride every time he saw the gold-stenciled letters on the door that read, Underwood Security Agency. To own one's own business in a town as competitive as Los Angeles was no small accomplishment; to make the kind of success of it that Bret had was little short of a miracle. He liked to remind himself of how well he had done—even though his present success still fell short of his original dreams, and even though he had done it all without the help of the perfect wife. But today, he didn't even glance at the lettering on the door. He was too distracted.

It should have come as no surprise to him that his secretary had already set up an ugly snow-flocked Christmas tree in the corner of the reception room and was now in the process of tacking miles of red garland across her desk, the walls and every other available surface.

"What's the rule around here, Miss Cranston?" he greeted her on the way to his office.

Linda Cranston was twenty-seven years old, blond, slim and California sexy. For that reason, Bret always addressed her as "Miss Cranston" and made sure every man on his staff did as well. She climbed down from the stepladder and quoted, "'No Christmas decorations before December 15.'"

"And what's the date today?"

"November 13."

"You're fired."

"Scrooge."

"Ho-ho-ho."

She followed him into his office with a handful of pink message slips. "You've got a dentist's appointment at noon, and Carol Weatherly wanted to know if you were free for lunch. I told her no, but I set up a tentative date for tomorrow...."

Bret glanced through the messages as he flipped on the monitor that connected him to the com center. Joel Phillips, night-shift supervisor, came onscreen, the row of consoles and operators who ensured the security of hundreds of exclusive, highly overpriced homes in the greater L.A. area forming a busy backdrop behind him.

"Morning, Joel," Bret said. "Anything?" He scrawled "no" across two party invitations, "yes" across a request to speak at a club luncheon, and "$500" across the bottom of a message from a charitable organization.

Joel grinned. "We had an intruder alarm at 4:15 from the Carringtons'. Turned out it was her boyfriend trying to get out the window when they thought they heard her husband come back early from a business trip. Boyfriend is fine. Husband is still in New York."

Bret returned the message slips to Linda. "Get Harold Syms on the phone for me, will you?" He turned back to Joel. "Anything else?"

"The usual. Gabe Riley's cat set off his motion detector again. We've told him to keep that cat locked up, but he insists the fault is in the system. I sent a man over there this morning. And Margaret Holloway swears she saw a man lurking outside her window last night. I told her there was no way anybody could get that close to her house without alerting every cop in L.A., but the poor old gal hasn't got anything else to do but worry, I guess. She wants more security.''

Bret nodded. ''Where would we be without the paranoia of the rich and famous, hmm? Go home, Joel, get some sleep.'' He grinned. ''And don't forget to set your security alarm. Mrs. Holloway's Peeping Tom might decide to try your house next.''

''Then he's in for a thrill,'' drawled Joel, and he switched off.

Linda came back in. ''Mr. Syms is out of the office, but Julia Lymon is on line one. They're taking a three-week cruise and want private patrols while they're gone. She wants you—'' Linda waggled an eyebrow at him meaningfully ''—to make the arrangements personally.''

Bret stifled a groan. Julia Lymon was a middle-aged, oversexed, Chanel-drenched dragon with too much money and too little self-restraint. He never left a meeting with her without feeling as though he were fleeing for his life—or his virtue, at the very least.

''Did you ever wake up one morning and discover you hate your job?'' he murmured.

Linda feigned innocence. ''Who me? Working for the sweetest guy in the world? Surely you jest.''

He winced. ''I guess I haven't exactly been a pussycat around here lately, have I?''

''More like a pit bull,'' Linda told him frankly. ''And it's going to be like this till after the holidays. Why don't you take a vacation?''

Bret glanced at the blinking light on the phone. ''No vacation. The crime rate always goes up during the holidays, you know that, and this year promises to be a beaut. Our client list will double."

She made a face. "What a cynic!"

"That's what pays the rent, babe. I don't make the statistics, I just—"

"Take advantage of them," she finished for him.

He looked at her steadily for a moment. "Just to show you what a sweetheart an old cynic can be, if you'll tell Julia Lymon I'm not in, you're not fired."

"If I tell her you're in the hospital, can *I* take a vacation?"

"In your dreams. Oh, and Miss Cranston—" he opened his brief case and pulled out the envelope from Johnson Web. "—send this over to Craig Notions with a letter. 'Enclosed are the documents relating to the Clayville property, which we discussed putting on the market last Thursday, et cetera, et cetera. You know what I mean."

She accepted the envelope. "I still don't understand why you're having an L.A. real-estate firm handle property in Indiana."

He shrugged. "There aren't a lot of wheeler-dealers in Clayville. There're over two hundred acres there, and I'll have a better chance of selling them if I get somebody who knows what he's doing."

"I don't know," she commented on her way out. "I'd think about it if I were you. A nice quiet farm in Indiana sounds to me like exactly what you need right now."

Insurrectionist that she was, Miss Cranston had hardly closed the door before she began to pipe Christmas music through the intercom. The song was

"Carol of the Bells," and it always reminded Bret of Dani.

Bret started to close his briefcase, but his eyes caught the plain white envelope on top. Slowly, he took it out but didn't read it again. He had every word memorized.

"Not fair, Dani," he muttered. He leaned back in his chair, balancing the envelope between two fingers and frowned at the opposite wall. He had enough on his hands this time of year trying to protect other people's peace of mind without a mystery like this unraveling his own. He didn't have time for dreary reminiscences of ten years ago; he didn't have room in his life to be sitting here, wondering how a small-town boy from Clayville, Indiana, had ended up in a suite of fifth-floor offices gleefully studying the rising crime rate and calling women "babe."

Maybe his secretary was right. He was a Scrooge and a cynic and it always got worse this time of year. But what could he expect after seven years in a business like this?

At first, building up a business, taking the chances, fighting off the competitors and scraping to make ends meet—it had all been exciting. Every day was a challenge, and he couldn't wait to get up in the mornings. But over the past few years, he had settled into a routine that was wearing on his nerves more and more each day, and the thought of the upcoming holiday season filled him with weariness and dread.

What he needed was to talk to Dani. Not about the letter—though how he could avoid mentioning it, he didn't know—but just to talk to her. There had never been a time in his life so bleak, so lonely or so desperate that talking to Dani hadn't made it right. From playground brawls to adolescent heartbreaks to those shocked, empty months after his divorce, somehow, the sound of her voice had always had the ability to put things in perspective, to reassure him, to make him laugh at himself again. He'd just give her a call, and if the matter of the letter came up...

His hand was on the telephone again, and then he stopped. Because he really didn't want to talk to Dani. He wanted to *see* her.

It was crazy. He didn't have time to go flying off to Indiana, especially not now. It would be cold in Indiana. He couldn't just desert his business on a moment's notice, leave his employees stranded, turn his back on the potential boom in new clients the holidays would bring, and all for the sake of something as stupid as a letter he was never supposed to read.

There's someone who loves you, Bret...

But he hadn't had a vacation in eight years, and it wasn't just the letter. There was the matter of the property he was trying to sell. Hadn't he been telling himself for years that what he really needed to do was make a trip out there and look at the place for himself? Now that he had decided to put it in the hands of a real-estate agent, *somebody* should look it over in person. Why put it off?

His hand was still on the receiver when the interoffice line buzzed. "Beechwood Promotions wants to know if you can handle the security for Neon Ecstasy on the fifteenth," Linda said.

"Who?"

"You know, the rock group. You're really out of it today. He needs six bodyguards for eighteen hours, and don't forget, you've promised to handle the Century Center party that night. And I've got Harold Syms on line three."

For the second time that morning, Bret stifled a groan. Guarding rock stars constituted hazardous duty for most of his staff; he practically had to force the men to draw lots in order to assign them. Without fail, he'd be called on site himself to deal with some trumped up problem or the other, and the Century Center people always expected him to show up and make a tour, just to reassure them everything was under control. Not to mention Harold Syms, who handled a dozen of Hollywood's most valuable—and temperamental—personalities; who knew which one of his "properties" Bret would be called upon to babysit this time? That was the trouble with building one's reputation on personalized service: everyone expected you to do the job personally.

Bret ran his fingers through his hair as the upcoming weeks began to look bleaker and bleaker. He looked at the letter lying on his desk. He tapped his fingers on the telephone receiver. Then he made a decision.

"Tell Beechwood we're booked," he said abruptly. "Confirm with Century. The guys can handle that without me. Tell Syms— Never mind, I'll tell him myself. And better cancel all my appointments for the next couple of weeks."

The silence on the other end of the line was stunned. "Are you okay?"

"No." Bret took the white envelope in his hand and then smiled. "I'm not okay. I need a vacation."

Chapter Two

"And that's the legend of the Christmas cactus," Dani finished, leaning one hip against the corner of her desk as she picked up the withered potted plant. "Every year, it blooms to remind us of what we're celebrating, and when it does, you know that Christmas has really come."

Four rows of semiattentive third-graders regarded the plant she held in her hand. Then Jimmy Skinner commented skeptically, "It looks dead to me."

"It's supposed to," she explained patiently. "All year long, it hibernates, and then at Christmastime, it suddenly comes to life again, and it's covered with flowers."

"How does it know when it's Christmas?" Melanie Kane wanted to know.

Dani smiled at her. "That's the miracle."

"What color are the flowers?"

"White, like Christmas snow."

Dani set the plant on her desk. Bret had sent the cactus to her five Christmases ago, and every year since, she had brought it up from the basement on December 1 and enthralled her class with the suspense of waiting for it to bloom. And every year, by the time the children left for the Christmas holidays, it had been covered with snowy white blossoms. The cactus had become one of the best parts of the season.

Jimmy said, "I think the bugs got to it. It's deader'n a doornail."

Dani tossed him a look of mild exasperation. There was always one in every class. "You just wait, Jimmy."

The bell rang, signaling a mad scramble for books and belongings. "All right," Dani called over the uproar. "Remember tomorrow starts the auditions for the school play, and start thinking about what you want to make for your parents for Christmas. Don't leave before you copy your homework off the blackboard!"

A few of the more conscientious students stopped to copy their homework; most of them rushed for the coat locker. Days were short this time of year and too precious to be wasted inside a schoolroom. Dani was in perfect sympathy, which was why, from the beginning of December to the end of the year, very little of academic value was built into her curriculum.

"Bye, Miss Griffin!"

"I want to make a birdhouse!"

"That's stupid—I want to make a bow and arrow!"

And Jimmy paused by Dani's desk, gave the cactus one last disgusted look and repeated, "Deader'n a doornail."

"Bye, Miss Griffin!"

"Goodbye, Karen. Be sure to have your mother look at that scrape on your knee. And, Tim, that hat goes on your head, not in your pocket!"

Tim pulled the stocking cap over his head as he ran out the door, only to rip if off and stuff it back into his pocket as soon as he thought he was out of sight.

Dani turned to her desk with a smile and a shake of her head, gathering up her papers to a chorus of "Bye, Miss Griffin" and "See you tomorrow!" In three minutes flat, the room was clear.

Though she was technically on duty until three-thirty, Dani had better things to do than spend the afternoon at school, too. At this time of year, she had approximately two hundred better things to do, and none of them involved filling out forms or picking up trash. She decided to come in early tomorrow to straighten the room, and the forms could wait until the beginning of the new year. She had just begun to give the blackboard a quick once-over with the eraser when a voice came from behind her.

"If I'd had a teacher who looked as good as you do, I might never have gotten out of third grade."

Dani turned. She dropped the eraser.

He stood leaning one shoulder against the door frame, sandy hair tousled by the wind, tweed over-coat open over a white cable-knit sweater and sleek gray slacks. He was wearing amber-tinted wire-framed glasses, and the faint bristle of blond beard on his jaw gave him a rakish, devil-may-care look. Broad shoulders, slim hips, perfect tan...

"Bret!" she cried, and flung herself at him.

She launched herself into his arms, throwing her arms around his neck and leaping up, winding her legs around his. He caught her, laughing, and stumbled backward against the desk. "Bret, you're here! What are you—"

"Get off me, you wicked woman, before I have to call the police!"

She sprang down lightly, and he held her at arm's length for a moment, flooded with a grin of pure pleasure, then he said, "Come here, funny face." And he pulled her to him again, hugging her hard.

They laughed again and hugged each other, then she broke away, striking out at him playfully. "Bret, you snake, sneaking up on me like that! And look at you, standing there as fresh as new money! What is this?" She lifted his tinted glasses and let them fall onto the bridge of his nose. "A new Hollywood trend or are you going blind in your old age?"

"A little of both," he admitted when she paused for breath.

She stood back with her hands on her hips. "Why didn't you tell me? When did you get in? What are you doing here?"

He looked at her, and he couldn't seem to stop grinning. She never changed. How was it that she never changed?

She was wearing a challis-print skirt, tan cowboy boots and a canary yellow blouse with big shoulders and a wing collar accented by a purple tapestry vest. The rich colors reflected the jewel tones of her eyes, which were sometimes violet and sometimes gray. Right now, her eyes were dancing with excitement. Her brown hair was wound into a flat braid and tied with a perky yellow bow at the back, just like the bows he used to take such delight in untying when he sat behind her in third grade. There was that same spattering of freckles across the nose she had always hated because it was too short, and her face was glowing with color just as it always did when she was happy. It was not a gorgeous face, or even a striking one—a little too round, with a broad forehead and cheeks that were quick to dimple—but her smile was as big as Indiana and could light up a room, or Bret's heart, in no more than an instant.

"What are you doing here?" she asked. Then her expression changed, quickening with concern as she took his face in one hand and examined it intently. "You look awful. Have you been driving all night? Is something wrong? What's wrong? Why did you come? Tell me what's wrong."

The letter lay like a guilty stain in his shirt pocket, and suddenly he knew he couldn't tell her why he had come. It was clear she knew nothing about his having the letter, and why embarrass her—or himself—by mentioning it now? She *would* think he was crazy if he told her he had driven eight hundred miles because of a letter she'd forgotten writing and had never meant for him to read. Besides, that wasn't really why he had come... not entirely.

"What?" he retorted, pulling his face away from her grip. "A guy can't come home for the holidays without getting the third degree?"

Her face lit up again. "Are you really? Are you going to stay?"

"For a while, at least. I've got some business to take care of, and I don't know—"

"That's great! I can't believe it, Christmas together just like old times! Bret, what a wonderful idea, but you could have *told* somebody, you know!" As she spoke, she had wound her arm through his and was leading him toward the door. "Mom is going to have a fit, she'll be so excited, but you'd better shave before you see her or she'll think you've gone and joined some weird religious group out in California—though as far as she's concerned, the whole state of California is a weird religious group—"

"Whoa, hold on!" He stopped her, laughing. "Come up for air, will you?"

"Can't help it, I'm too excited." She tugged on his arm impatiently. "This is perfect. If you don't take all day about it, you can wash up and change, and we can still get downtown in time to help string the lights. And tonight is the first bonfire down at the lake—"

"Change into what? You're looking at the only clothes I have suitable for this North Pole you call home, and I had to stop at Sears in Omaha to buy the coat. I haven't even checked into the motel yet. And I hope this little burg has come up with something better than the Route Fifty Inn in the past five years because—"

"We'll go shopping later," she decreed cheerfully. "First you've got to drive me home. And for heaven's sake, will you *tell* me what possessed the city slicker to take a down-home holiday all of a sudden? What's been going on, anyway? What happened to that decorator you were seeing—did you ever get rid of her?

Last I heard, she had roped you into taking her to that banquet...."

Laughing, Bret scooped up Dani's coat and draped it over her shoulders as they walked outside. On the way, he told her how he had dumped the decorator—politely, of course—on the night of the banquet. Dani told him he was a jerk, and he agreed he probably was. He ended up driving her home even though it meant he would have to take her back to school the next morning to pick up her car. Because they were laughing and talking so much, it didn't occur to him to do anything else, and because Dani was, as always, as uncontrollable as wildfire and just as contagious.

DANI DID NOT LIVE WITH her parents, but her living arrangements were the next best thing, and for an unmarried woman in a town as small as Clayville, the only acceptable compromise between independence and propriety. Her parents still lived in the century-old farmhouse where she had grown up. They had never worked the land on any large scale and over the years, the property had been reduced from hundreds of acres to twelve. Dani's home was a converted barn at the end of the long driveway that led to the main farmhouse. Her father had restored and redesigned the structure into what Dani's friends called a dream cottage. For Dani, the best thing about it was the hundred or so yards of hedge-lined drive that separated her house from her parents' home.

Of course, Bret could not just drop her off in front of her house, so he proceeded up the drive to the farmhouse. Harold Griffin's hand was evident in the well-kept, restored and improved main house, too, and it had always been a matter of some pride to Dani that theirs was the most attractive house on the road. Dani's father owned the local lumberyard, but Dani often thought that, had he not inherited the business from his father, he might have gone on to be one of the great architects of the time—or at the very least, a highly successful contractor. But Harold contented himself with "fixing up" their place or other peoples', and when neighbors came into the store asking him for advice on how to add a porch or modernize a bathroom, he would likely as not go out and do the job himself—for free.

Dani pulled Bret up the three steps and across the wide porch at a semirun, calling, "Mom, company!" before she even got the door open. Bret paused in the slate-tiled front hall to take off his coat and let the sights and scents of home rush over him, pushing him back through three decades of memories.

The house smelled of something sweet and spicy baking in the kitchen, with the undertone of that dark furniture polish his own mother had always used on the family heirlooms. The starched lace curtains at the front windows hadn't changed in twenty years, and neither had the overstuffed chair in the living room or the braided rugs on the hardwood floor. Bret remembered when Dani's father had caught the big bass that was now stuffed and mounted over the fireplace and when Bret, at age sixteen, had helped the older man install the flying staircase that had been rescued from an old church tower. He had learned more than he ever wanted to know about building that summer.

"Bret Underwood, as I live and breathe!"

Anne Griffin stood at the threshold that led to the kitchen, and Bret went toward her with his arms open. "Miss Annie," he said. "It's good to see you!"

"What on earth—" But she interrupted her own exclamation to hug him, and Bret thought Thomas Wolfe must have been crazy in saying you can't go home again. Nothing had ever felt more like home to Bret.

Anne Griffin was a short, sporty-looking woman with straight brown hair cut in a pageboy. She had grown a little plump over the years, but that only gave her a more motherly look. She was wearing a gray sweatsuit and her husband's oversize white socks, and though there was presently a smear of flour on her oven-flushed cheeks, Bret knew she had just as soon be out chopping wood or replacing broken shingles as baking a cake.

She held his shoulders and looked at him, beaming. "Well, I couldn't be more surprised if the Archangel Gabriel just walked into my front room! Dani, why didn't you say something? And here the house is a mess—"

"Oh, Mom, get real!" Dani made a face. "Your house wouldn't be a mess after an earthquake, flood and fire. Besides, Bret's family."

Annie touched his cheek, looking worried. "Are you growing a beard? You haven't joined some cult, have you?"

Dani's eyes twinkled, and Bret replied soberly, "No ma'am. I've been driving all night."

"You know better than that! Pull over every two hours, that's what your daddy always said, and you should listen to him. I'll tell you something else, you're too thin—all California folks are, aren't they? It's from eating all that seaweed and tofu and whatnot, but we'll fix that! Now, you just give me a minute to get your room in order—"

"No, wait, I didn't come to impose. I planned on staying at a motel—"

Anne gave him a look filled with patient disgust. "Don't talk nonsense. Do you want to end up with some kind of disease? You're staying here. Go on out to the kitchen and make yourself something to eat. I'll just put fresh sheets on the bed and straighten up the bureau. Dani, check that pie in the oven for me, will you?"

Bret watched Anne disappear up the stairs, shaking his head helplessly. "Your mother..."

"You didn't really think you were going to get to stay in a motel, did you?" Dani said over her shoulder on the way to the kitchen. "Folks would think we'd turned you out—we'd never live it down."

"Yeah, I guess you're right," Bret admitted ruefully. "And your mom's cooking beats diner food anyday. Do you think I protested enough?"

"Hardly enough to be polite."

The kitchen was big and airy; the floors and one wall were covered with age-darkened brick Harold Griffin had scavenged from a riverfront warehouse, and there was a big brick fireplace that, in Bret's youth, had been boarded over to conserve heat. Now it was open and a couple of logs crackled with merry flames, adding the scent of seasoned oak to those of cinnamon and cloves that filled the room.

Bret got a glass from a cabinet and poured himself some milk, just as he had done when he was twelve. "Funny, I never can remember where the glasses are in my own house."

"That's because you keep going through decorators so fast." Dani opened the oven door and slid out the rack with a mittened hand. A perfectly crusted pie sat bubbling on it, but apparently, it was not quite brown enough because Dani closed the door again and tossed the oven mitt onto the stovetop.

Bret hoisted himself to the kitchen counter and helped himself to the contents of the cookie jar. "This place never changes," he said, looking around contentedly.

"Sure it does." Dani scooped up a couple of cookies and sat down at the breakfast table, swinging her feet onto the opposite chair. "We've got cable now."

She took a bite out of the cookie and regarded him with alert, bright-eyed interest. "So," she demanded. "What's going on?"

Dani knew Bret too well to imagine that he had left his business and driven all this way just to spend the holidays in his old hometown. But she also knew him well enough to have seen this coming for some time now. Over the past few months, she had been able to read the restlessness and dissatisfaction in his phone conversations and notes. He was working harder and enjoying it less, but that was only part of the problem. The rest of the problem he would tell her in his own time . . . or when he figured out what it was himself.

But that time was apparently not now. He bit into the cookie and answered, "I've decided to put the old place on the market. Thought I'd come down and look it over, see what needs to be done, that sort of thing."

Dani waved a dismissive hand. "You've been talking about selling the place for years. You're never going to do it."

"Oh, yes, I am. What do I need to keep paying taxes on it for? The rent I get barely pays the upkeep. So I listed it last week."

She lifted an eyebrow. "No kidding? Well, good luck finding a buyer. Nobody around here has that kind of money."

Bret glanced down at the half-eaten cookie. "I wasn't thinking about anybody around here. Actually, I listed it with an L.A. broker. He thinks he might be able to stir up some corporate interest."

Dani stared at him. He sounded serious. "What do you mean, 'corporate interest'?"

"You know, shopping malls, office complexes, resort hotels . . ."

She gave a little bark of laughter. "You nut, you had me worried there for a minute!"

"What, you don't think I can do it?"

"Yeah, right, the minute you strike oil on the south forty." She smiled at him, eyes twinkling. "You know what I think? I think you just missed me, and all this business about selling the farm is an excuse."

"Well, in that case, I'd better call the Saudis and tell them to cancel their inspection tour." And his face softened. "Yeah, I missed you, skunk. I want to know what's going on with you."

There was a gentle intensity to his question that touched Dani's heart. It didn't matter why Bret had come or what excuse he had used; he was here. He had always known when she needed to talk to him; he had always managed to somehow be there for her just as he was now. She had never needed her best friend more than she did at this moment, and the funny thing was that she hadn't even realized it until he was there.

But as good as it was to have him here, to know that he was ready to listen as soon as she was ready to talk, Dani was also, strangely, a little uncomfortable. She didn't know where to begin.

Fortunately—or perhaps not so fortunately—her mother did it for her. "Dani," she called down the stairs. "I forgot to tell you—Todd called. He has to work late and won't be able to take you to the bonfire tonight. He wants you to call him back."

"Todd?" Bret frowned sharply. "Who's he?"

"Okay, Mom," Dani called back. "Thanks!" And to Bret she said, "I told you about Todd. He's the new editorial manager at the newspaper."

Bret was still frowning skeptically. "I don't think so. I would've remembered somebody named *Todd*." He made the name sound like something nice people didn't repeat in mixed company.

She scowled irritably as she got up and took his empty glass, rinsing it under the faucet. "I did, too. You just never listen. And what's wrong with his name? It's a perfectly nice name."

"For an eighteen-year-old beach boy, or maybe the cover model on *Musclebound*."

"Good Lord, where do you come up with these things? You don't even know him!"

Bret was watching her closely—too closely—and it made her cheeks sting, to her further annoyance. She twisted the tap off with a snap and dried her hands.

"So, what's the deal?" His voice was too mild. "How'd you meet this dude? Are you sleeping with him?"

"I never sleep with anybody who lives within a twenty-mile radius of this town, you know that," she replied airily, but her cheeks were only getting hotter.

"You are!" he declared softly. "You're hot and heavy with a guy named Todd! Well, this is going to take some looking into."

"You're impossible!" She tossed the towel at him.

The teasing faded from his eyes and was replaced by a look she couldn't quite read as he took another cookie from the jar, then popped it into his mouth with a gesture too studied to be casual. "So," he said after a moment, "are you going to tell me about him?"

Dani hesitated and then realized that as much as she had wanted to talk to Bret about this only a few moments ago, she really did not want to think about Todd now. And at the same time, she realized something that should have disturbed her, but didn't: she was glad Todd canceled their date for tonight because that meant she would get to go to the bonfire with Bret.

She said, "Later," and gave him a gentle push off the counter. "Right now, you'd better get moving—we've got Christmas lights to string!"

Bret silently accepted her wish to change the subject as, being Bret, he would. But he gave a groan of protest as he sprang to the floor. "Have mercy, girl, I've been driving sixteen hours straight. What I need is a shower and a long nap."

"What you need," she corrected, pushing him toward the door, "is to get in the spirit. Only twenty-four days left till Christmas, and Santa needs every helping hand he can get."

"Ah, Dani, don't start with me. You know I hate all that holiday stuff."

She stopped and stared at him. "You do not! You love it."

"I hate it," he insisted. "I hate stringing lights and chopping trees and standing in the freezing rain singing 'Deck the Halls' and God, do I hate shopping. So please, just do me a favor and leave me out of all the holiday falderol, okay?"

She continued to stare at him as though he were an alien species, then abruptly dismissed it. "You're lying. You love it, and you know you do."

"Hate it. Always have and always will."

"You love it. Now come on, we're going to miss all the fun."

Bret tried to remember a time when he had ever considered standing atop a cherry picker in the icy wind and stringing Christmas lights from lampposts fun, but he couldn't. Still, it was easier to pretend resignation than to argue with Dani, so he let her push him out the door.

And the single consolation was that, no matter how cold it was and no matter how tired he was, he was spending the afternoon with Dani. She had a way of making nothing else matter, and he was glad he had come home.

Chapter Three

Clayville, Indiana, was one of those postcard-perfect towns that dotted the Midwest. "Downtown" consisted of three intersecting streets six blocks long with a steepled church at the intersection square. There were benches outside the bank where old men really played checkers, and a small park shaded by an enormous spreading elm tree and accented by a granite watering trough that these days was more frequently used by birds than horses.

The population—excluding those in the outlying rural area—was just over six hundred, and every one of those six hundred people knew not only their neighbors' names, but their neighbors' secrets. It was the kind of place that had been built on barn-raisings and quilting bees, and the sense of community had flowed effortlessly into the twentieth century.

In Clayville, one did not have the option of being uninvolved. When the one-room police station and jail was struck by lightning and burned to the ground, Harold Griffin donated the lumber and everyone pitched in to rebuild. When the school budget was too small to afford computers, local merchants and businessmen ran contests and drives until enough money was raised for four new computers for the upper grades. And when the first of December rolled around, every able-bodied man and woman with an hour to spare donated that time to dragging out the boxes of town Christmas decorations, uncoiling wires and rolls of garland, hanging lights and draping greenery across the streets.

And in Clayville, nobody ever forgot who you were. Bret was greeted as though he had only been away on a short vacation, and before he knew it, Dani's father had slapped a pair of work gloves into his hands and assigned him—of course—to the bucket of the cherry picker.

"Some welcome-home party!" Bret called down to Dani, who was sorting through a pickup truck full of evergreen boughs and wreaths.

She grinned up at him, her cheeks chapped and her hair tossed by the wind. "You ain't seen nothing yet!"

When they were younger, Bret and Dani used to watch this same ritual every year, resentful of the childish tasks they were assigned, like tying bows on wreaths and replacing light bulbs, impatient for the time they would be grown-up enough to do the important jobs. Now other children tied the bows and other grown-ups admonished them to be careful not to break that box of ornaments. Watching it all from his bird's-eye view, Bret felt a weird and uncomfortable sense of déjà vu.

He still hated it. The cold stung his ears and crept inside his thin Italian-leather loafers to freeze his toes. He couldn't imagine anything more stupid than risking life and limb and electrical shock to hang strings of red and green lights across a main thoroughfare. But when twilight came and the switch was turned on to a clamor of cheers and applause, even Bret had to admit it was all kind of pretty...in a tacky, small-town way.

"I can't believe I let you talk me into this," he said, rubbing the small of his back. "Every muscle in my body aches, and I've got blisters on my hands, and I can't feel my toes. Can we go home now?"

"Only sissies get blisters," Dani retorted, slipping her arm around his waist. "That's what you get for living the soft life. And, of course, we're not going home. Now's our reward for working so hard—the bonfire."

"Which you've, no doubt, volunteered to build," he returned wryly, and she laughed.

"Now, Bret, isn't this fun? Aren't you having a good time?"

"On a scale of one to ten," he answered, "with dental surgery being a one—this ranks maybe two and a half."

"What's ten?"

"Sex."

They walked back to his car with their arms around each other's waists. Bret walked close to Dani for warmth, and because he liked the way she smelled in the crisp, early-night air—like cinnamon and vanilla.

"So, what would you be doing if you were at home?" she asked.

He chuckled. "It wouldn't be a ten, I'll tell you that."

"What?" She slanted a dancing glance at him. "I'm disappointed. I always pictured you wallowing in that wild every-night's-a-party, Southern California lifestyle. You know, wearing a purple silk kimono and sipping Dubonnet and filling the hot tub with bubble bath...."

"Only on alternate weekends."

"So what *would* you be doing?"

"As a matter of fact, I'd probably still be in the office." And it surprised Bret to realize that he hadn't thought about the office once all day. That was gratifying, he supposed, though it was scant compensation for stiff muscles and frostbite.

"And then?"

He opened the car door for her. "Then I'd probably pick up some Chinese food on the way home, watch the late news and go to bed."

"Wow. Even I do better than that."

Bret couldn't help wondering, then, just how she did. And he wondered about Todd.

As he slid behind the wheel, it occurred to Bret how little they really did know about each other these days. There had been a time when every detail of her life, big and small, had been a part of his. They had never had to ask what the other was thinking because they always knew. And they never had to write down secrets because, between the two of them, there simply were no secrets.

But something was lost in the translation over long distance. He told her about his loves and losses, his triumphs and defeats, just as he always had. She told him about her hopes and dreads, just as she always had. They exchanged funny stories and sad news, they gossiped and they philosophized, and yet...something was missing, and he hadn't even realized it until now.

He reached across the seat and squeezed her hand. "I've missed you, sweetheart," he said simply.

She looked surprised for just a moment, then she smiled and wrapped her gloved fingers around his. He held her hand all the way to the lake.

The annual bonfire was the first official event of the Christmas season. Women had been baking and simmering their prize-winning specialties all day, and as soon as it was dark, families would pack up their covered dishes, drive through town to "ooh" and "ahh" over the Christmas lights, then rendezvous at the lake. A select committee had been working on the bonfire since just before sunset, and by dark, a respectable blaze was shooting sparks into the air. Beneath the covered pavilion, casseroles were kept warm over Sterno pots, and baked goods of every description were spread out on picnic tables. Barbecue pits were fired up for roasting hot dogs and German sausages, and there was always plenty of caramel popcorn and candied apples. Neighbors filled their plates and gossiped back and forth. Children, delighted by the spectacle of the bonfire and the opportunity to play outside after dark, ran wild while their parents constantly shouted at them to stay away from the lake and not get too close to the fire.

More marriage proposals and other, slightly less-acceptable, romantic encounters had taken place at the annual bonfire than at any other time of the year. There was something intoxicating about a cold, star-studded night with a centerpiece of leaping flames bathing faces and figures in soft yellow light; something intimate and even a little pagan about the lush scent of evergreens and tangy wood smoke. Voices were always a little louder, laughter more uninhibited, and the sense of secrecy and adventure inherent in sneaking away from the crowd for a stolen kiss or a few moments of shared body warmth always made the experience doubly exciting.

"Boy, does this bring back memories," Bret murmured as he got out of the car.

"Carla McBride," Dani teased him.

He gave her a withering look. "I never came out here with Carla McBride."

"Then you were the only boy in town who didn't."

"Whatever happened to her, anyway?"

"She married a shoe salesman from Indianapolis, had five children and got as fat as a cow."

"See? I knew there was a good reason I never came out here with her."

"Dani! Hi!" Mary Witt waved to her, a parka-clad two-year-old in tow as she made her way across the snow-spotted ground toward them. "Is that— Good heavens, it can't be! Bret Underwood?"

It wasn't long after that that other people spotted Bret. Those who hadn't had the chance to do so welcomed him home and barraged him with questions, someone thrust a cup of hot chocolate into his hand, and someone else insisted he come have a bite of her mincemeat pie and tell her if it wasn't just like the recipe his own mother had made famous county wide.

Dani sneaked away to help Mary carry her two casseroles to the pavilion.

"Imagine that," Mary said, hoisting her son on her hip and tucking the casserole under her arm. "What do you suppose he's doing back here?"

"Here, let me take that. I can carry both of them." Dani took the casserole from Mary and stacked it on top of the one she already had.

"Isn't he some kind of important businessman in California? Banking or something?"

"Security agency. You know, locks and burglar alarms and body guards?"

"Oh." Mary seemed momentarily confused. "Well, anyway, I hear he's as rich as God."

Dani shook her head in pure amazement at how tangled small-town gossip could get—even though she was sure she herself, at one time or another, had probably been a party to it. "Richer than you and me, maybe, but he's no Howard Hughes. Not that I know of, anyway."

"I guess there must be a lot of call for that kind of thing in Los Angeles," Mary mused. "All those movie stars and such."

"Bret always was smart," Dani agreed, and was aware of a touch of motherly pride in her voice.

Mary glanced at her shrewdly. "So where's Todd tonight?"

Dani felt a small prickle of guilt that she had forgotten to return his call. "Working late. You know how it is."

"Does he know about, umm, Bret?"

Dani stopped and lifted the casseroles out of harm's way as a group of squealing children raced past, but she did not miss the insinuating tone in Mary's voice. She chose to ignore it. "Bret just got in this afternoon. I haven't had a chance to introduce them."

"Now *that* should be interesting," Mary murmured.

Dani couldn't ignore that. "What do you mean?"

They had reached the pavilion, where lines were already forming for food and compliments were being shouted back and forth as people warmed their hands around cups of cider and called out requests for Miss Annabelle's rice pudding or Laura Crow's three-bean casserole. Bret was, of course, in one of those lines, surrounded by high school friends and beaming matrons. Mary lowered her voice conspiratorially as she glanced at him.

"Come on, Dani, you and Bret have been an item as long as I can remember. What's Todd going to think when he finds out the competition is in town?"

"Mary Witt, for heaven's sake!" Dani set the casseroles on the table and dodged the groping fist of Mary's son as he grabbed for her braid. "Hi, Mrs. Carpenter. Everything looks great, doesn't it?"

She lowered her voice as she said to Mary, "We were not an item! Bret's always been like a brother to me."

"If you say so," Mary replied innocently, but her eyes were twinkling with a secret mirth as she turned to uncover her casserole. "Still, I think Bret's even better-looking now than he was in high school, don't you? If Todd's got any sense at all, he's going to be jealous."

Dani liked to think that the color that fanned her cheeks was due to nothing more than irritation with Mary's teasing, for she had always blushed too easily. But the truth was, she was remembering a time when she hadn't thought of Bret as a brother at all, and whether the blush was caused by embarrassment or regret, she couldn't be sure.

She stole a quick glance at him through the crowd. He was talking to one of the girls they had grown up with, and even though the woman in question was happily married and pregnant, Dani could see how she responded to his smile and his joking banter. In fact, most of the people surrounding Bret were female, many of them single, but Dani told herself that wasn't too surprising. After all, it wasn't every day that the women of Clayville were treated to the sight of a man with professionally styled hair and Italian shoes. The home-town-boy-made-good was bound to generate a little excitement. But it wasn't as though he was a football star or a politician or anything, and it began to occur to Dani that those women were seeing something in Bret she wasn't...or perhaps something she had always known but thought no one else did.

Of course, Bret was good-looking. She had begun to understand that about the time they were juniors in high school when, all of a sudden, Bret's ears didn't seem too big for his head anymore and his arms and legs weren't too long for his body and the face that had once seemed thin and angular became masculine and arresting. The transformation had taken Dani by surprise, but it was more than the metamorphosis of an awkward adolescent into a striking young man. The confidence and charm Bret had always had evolved into style, a distinctive way of moving and talking and laughing that complemented his handsome profile and strong masculine form and set him head and shoulders above his peers. Somehow, Dani had always thought no one appreciated that but her.

Looking back, she realized she had had a dreadful crush on Bret those last couple of years of high school. But it was so difficult to allow changes in a relationship that had remained virtually impenetrable for all their lives. She hadn't even recognized the emotion for what it was at the time. She made excuses to be with him, she dressed for him, she wore her hair for him, she even cancelled dates with other boys to spend an evening doing nothing but watching television with Bret . . . and why not? He was the most popular boy in school, and all the other girls were jealous when she went out with him. Plus, he was her best friend.

It was only toward the end of that last wonderful, frantic, desperately intense summer between high school and college that she began to realize that Bret had become more to her than a friend. By the end of the summer, they would be going their separate ways, they would be apart for the first time in their lives, and Dani could not imagine surviving without him. Convinced he was the only man she could ever love, she had spent the summer torn between ecstasy and despair, her misery further compounded by the fact that Bret was completely unaware of how her feelings for him had changed. She would never know what might have happened had she somehow gotten up the courage to tell him, but it didn't matter. Toward the end of the summer, they had a fight—she couldn't even remember what it was about now—and she had been only too happy to flounce off to Indiana State on her own, while Bret went on to Berkeley.

Their relationship was too strong, of course, to be destroyed by one fight, and over the course of their college years, they once again settled into the comfortable, dependable roles of best friends and confidants. When Dani thought about the grand passion she had nursed for him that last summer, it was with the embarrassment of a newly formed adult for the childish things of the past. Bret was her lifelong friend and closer than a brother, but he had his life and she had hers, and all those silly romantic fantasies were long since forgotten.

She had really believed that, until she saw him again the summer after they graduated—Bret with a degree in business administration and she with one in education. There he was, tall and tan with sun-streaked hair and twinkling hazel eyes, as familiar as childhood but as fresh as tomorrow, and she had fallen helplessly, hopelessly in love with him all over again. And even though she fought it, though she tried to deny it and devoted every ounce of her energy to convincing herself it wasn't so and to preventing him from finding out, this was no girlish crush. This was love, quiet and genuine and desperately real. But he was in love with another woman.

Dani never told him, and at the end of the summer, he married someone else and broke Dani's heart for the last time.

It was all so long ago, a mere thread in the rich tapestry of history they had woven between them, and looking at him now, Dani felt a little uncomfortable with the memories. She was thirty-three years old and liked to think she knew something of life; loves had come and gone and so had heartbreak, disappointment and failure—for both of them. They were different people from those they had been twenty years ago, or even ten. Childish infatuations and secret devotions belonged to the past, and she was very happy to keep them there. Still, she couldn't help wondering what would have happened if, at any juncture, her relationship with Bret had taken a different course.

Her mother called to her, and the real world burst the bubble of speculation and memories. For the next hour and a half, as she dished out food and drink, all Dani saw of Bret was a glimpse through the crowd.

The traditional climax of the evening was the ritual tossing of the final logs on the fire, and when everyone agreed that the blaze was roaring as brightly as it could possibly get, they would all gather round to sing Christmas carols. That was, for Dani, one of the most moving and uplifting moments of the entire season, and this year, it would be doubly so because Bret was here. She couldn't remember how long it had been since the two of them had stood side by side with the fire stinging their cheeks while the clear, sweet voices of the entire community were lifted on the winter's air. But she knew her best memories were of nights like this, cold hands warming each other's, collars turned up against the wind, their voices straining to outdo each other with "Deck the Halls" or "The First Noel."

She went in search of Bret while the men were heaving the last of the big logs on the fire to the enthusiastic cheers of the onlooking crowd. She found him talking to Lenore Skinner who, with her husband George and son Jimmy, had tenanted Bret's farm for the past four years.

"Of course, we're not going to terminate the lease," Bret was saying, "and you'll have plenty of notice before I sell. But people will be coming out to look at the place from time to time, and I thought you should know what my plans were."

Lenore Skinner smiled weakly. She was a thin, work-worn woman in a shabby cotton coat that last year had belonged to someone else. Not even her attempt at a polite smile made her look more attractive or less tired. "You really should talk to my husband about this, Mr. Underwood."

Bret glanced around. "Well, I was hoping I'd get to see him tonight."

Lenore smoothed her hands on her coat nervously. "No. He couldn't come. I think he's coming down with a bug."

"Maybe I could drive out in a couple of days. But meanwhile, I don't want you to worry. You've been fine tenants over the years, and I'll do everything possible to make the transition easy for you."

Lenore shook her head, no longer smiling. "It doesn't matter, Mr. Underwood." Her voice sounded weary. "It's probably for the best, anyhow. George and me...well, I don't reckon we'd be staying on long after the first of the year, anyhow.''

She walked away, and Bret looked after her, puzzled. Dani came up to him. ''They've been having a hard time,'' she explained quietly. ''George Skinner doesn't know anything but farming, and you know that land has never been good for much more than weeds. With the drought the last couple of years, they haven't been able to even grow that. He's tried to hold down other jobs, but the plant over in Centerville started laying off last year and, well...'' She finished the sentence with a shrug.

Bret frowned. ''I'm sorry to hear that. I know they've been late with the rent a lot, but it never bothered me, and I just figured they came up short sometimes, like people do. I didn't know it was that serious.''

''The rent comes mostly from the tips Lenore makes at Harry's Café out on Route 20. She had two jobs for a while—one at the café and another at the dime store in town. Then Ruby Likes decided she couldn't afford full-time help at the store, so they're back to living off just tips.''

''Well, I guess selling the farm is going to be good for them, too,'' Bret said. ''It'll give them a chance to get out of this place and start over.''

Something about the way he said that disturbed Dani—so easily, so matter-of-factly, almost callously. Did he really think people like the Skinners could just pull up roots and start over? Did he really think being forced out of one's home could be good for *anyone?*

But a quick glance at his face assured her that Bret did not mean to be callous or self-serving, and wasn't even aware of how his response had sounded. Everything had always been easy for Bret, the solution to any problem simple and straightforward, and he just didn't understand that it wasn't always so for other people. He had been living in Los Angeles so long, he had forgotten what it was like in the real world. He would remember soon enough.

Meanwhile, the whole issue of the Skinners was academic because he would never be able to sell that farm.

Dani said, "The worst part is, their money problems are only the tip of the iceberg. Their son, Jimmy, is in my class, and I gather there's real trouble at home. George Skinner wasn't sick tonight—he just doesn't go out anymore. Not to church, not to town, especially not anywhere with his wife. He just sits at home, with a bottle most likely, and watches that old black-and-white television day in and day out."

Bret gave a small shake of his head. "Welcome to Norman Rockwell's America, huh?"

The shadow of depression crept toward them, threatening to ruin a perfect evening, and Dani pushed it back determinedly. Not on Bret's first night home. Not at her favorite gathering of the year, and not when they had so much to celebrate. She wound her arm through his and said cheerfully, "Come on, they're about to start the Christmas carols."

Bret groaned. "Dani, I'm freezing. Couldn't we just—"

"It's warm by the fire." She tugged on his arm.

"But Christmas carols! Anything but Christmas carols! It's not even the middle of December and I'm already up to my eyeballs in Christmas carols. Can't we just skip it?"

She dropped his arm, staring at him. "We certainly cannot! What's wrong with you anyway? How'd you turn into such a boring old man?"

"Scrooge," he corrected. "My secretary calls me a Scrooge, and it's a reputation I've worked hard to earn." But he could tell by the expression on Dani's face that she was not amused, so he compromised. "Couldn't we just sit in the car and listen? I'm not kidding. If I stand out in this cold any longer, I'm going to turn into a popsicle. Buy you some caramel popcorn," he coaxed with a grin.

He could tell she was disappointed, but she relented. They went to the car with a bag of caramel popcorn between them, and he ran the engine for a few minutes to warm the interior.

Dani decided after a while that a break in the tradition wasn't entirely bad. The windows were steamed up, turning the inside of the automobile into a cozy, private niche through which muted sounds of carolers were still perfectly audible. It was nice being alone with Bret, away from the crowd, munching on caramel popcorn and not feeling compelled to talk. Thinking, perhaps, a little too much about the past, but they were good memories.

She glanced across the bucket seat at him. "The first time you ever kissed me was here, do you remember?"

"Hmm." His voice sounded lazy and content. "Do you know, if cars had had bucket seats back then, I probably wouldn't have kissed a girl till I was twenty."

She chuckled in agreement. "You were the first, you know."

"The first what?"

"Boy to kiss me."

"Yeah. You were the first girl I kissed, too."

She was surprised. "Really? I never knew that."

"That good, was I?" he returned smugly.

"As far as I was concerned, you were." She popped a kernel of caramel popcorn into her mouth. "Too bad you couldn't have been the first for other things, too."

His eyebrow shot up in a pretense of shock. "Why, Dani Griffin, I can't imagine what you mean."

She shifted a little uncomfortably in her seat. "Well, anybody would've been better than that big jerk of a quarterback I thought I was so in love with in college."

"Pretty bad, huh?"

"The first time?" She shuddered. "Awful. God, nineteen-year-old girls can be stupid."

A silence fell, and in its wake, an awkwardness developed that was as unexpected as it was inexplicable. They had always talked as freely about sex as they had about everything else; never had embarrassment or constraint gotten in the way. Why should this time be different?

Maybe it was the close intimacy of the car making Bret's long, lean body seem to fill even more space than it usually did. Maybe it was the opaque windows and the singers just outside, heard but not seen, and the fresh, poignant memories of adolescent experimentation. Maybe it was in the way she said it: *Too bad you couldn't have been the first...*

And maybe it was because she had accidentally, involuntarily, almost told him more than she ever wanted him to know.

It was Bret who broke the awkwardness, as he could always be counted on to do, by delving into the popcorn bag and commenting, "I hope it got better over the years."

Dani relaxed. "Oh, sure. Doesn't everything? All it takes is finding the right guy."

Bret asked, "Like Todd?"

Dani looked at him. His voice was deliberately casual, but his expression was just as deliberate and trying very hard not to appear so. He was half-turned from her, pretending to be very interested in what he could not see through the front windshield, munching on popcorn, affecting a total lack of concern. But the hazy firelight reflected on his jaw and outlined a certain tightness there, played in his eyes and illuminated a tense expectation he could not entirely conceal.

Dani said impatiently, "For heaven's sake, Bret, you've been dying to ask me about Todd since this afternoon. Why don't you just come right out and say so?"

He turned to her, his eyes sober and concealing nothing. "I thought I had."

And so he had. Dani had evaded him then, and she hadn't known why. Now she did, but it was too late.

There was no way she could avoid telling her best friend the most important secret of her life.

But suddenly, it was the last thing in the world she wanted to do.

The carolers began singing "Good King Wenceslas." Dani wished with all her being she were out there with them, instead of trapped in this car having this conversation with Bret. But she took a breath, and without looking at him, she said, "I've been seeing him for about eight months. He's—he's great Bret, really smart and fun to be with, and he has this fantastic sense of commitment...you know, to the world, the environment and society as a whole. He's the newspaper editor—I told you that didn't I?—and you wouldn't believe the changes he's made. It's like a real newspaper now instead of that twice-monthly rag we used to have. He's on the town council, too, but he's not really a politician—not that he wouldn't make a great one, he just doesn't play those games. But he's involved in everything. I mean, he's only been here two years, but already people know that if there's a job to be done, they can count on Todd Renshaw to do it."

She paused for breath, still not looking at him, and Bret said guardedly, "He sounds like a terrific guy."

"He is," she agreed quickly. "You'd really like him."

Bret waited.

She reached for more popcorn, changed her mind and folded her hands in her lap. "He's asked me to marry him," she said. She pulled at the fingers of her gloves, straightened them again and forced herself to look at Bret. "And I think I'm going to say yes."

Chapter Four

Bret drove Dani home and rather absently refused her invitation to come inside for cocoa. As he went up the warmly lit steps of the main house, he realized he had arrived before the elder Griffins and that he didn't have a key—but the front door was unlocked, as he should have known it would be. With a rueful shake of his head, he went inside, for what should have been a sign of trust and welcome only served to remind Bret how little he belonged here.

It would be rude to go to bed before his hosts arrived home, but suddenly, every bone in Bret's body ached with fatigue. He scrawled a note on the back of a sheet torn from his address book—"Exhausted. Made myself at home. Thanks again! Bret"—and propped it up on the mantel. He made his way upstairs to the room that had always been his, and wondered how much of his exhaustion was physical and how much was sheer emotional shock.

He couldn't remember exactly what he had said to Dani following her startling announcement—something snappy and clever about old-maid schoolteachers, most likely, followed by a witty assault of teasing, which was exactly what she would expect from him. Pretty soon, she lost that uncomfortable, anxious look and started to respond in kind. When he left her, she was laughing. Bret was reeling.

The room had not changed much since he was a boy and had stayed over for early-morning hunting trips with Dani's dad or had stayed late after a party when the roads were too icy to drive home. The bed was an old oak four-poster, the bureau, a slightly mismatched turn-of-the-century piece, the curtains forest green and the braided rug faded with washing. It was always a little chilly up here, even with the furnace Harold Griffin had put in in 1972, and the bed was piled high with hand-made quilts. It had always been a comfortable room to Bret, a familiar room.

In deference to the quilts, Bret kicked off his shoes before lying back on the bed. He folded his arms beneath his head and stared up at the ceiling. Dani, getting married. Well, what had he expected? That she would wait for him forever?

Wait for him... He frowned at the unexpected slip and couldn't imagine where it had come from. It wasn't as though he wanted to marry her or had ever even thought about it. But neither had he planned on her marrying somebody else, and the possibility was so alien, so new and surprising, that it was going to take him longer than one evening to adjust to it. No, he didn't want to marry her. But he didn't want to lose his best friend, either.

This must have been exactly the way Dani felt when he told her he was getting married ten years ago.

And the irony was, of course, that it was a ten-year-old letter that had brought him back here now, only to find the same scene being played out again—in reverse.

Slowly, he withdrew the letter from his pocket and looked at it for a long time without opening it. Well, this answered one question, anyway. Dani certainly hadn't meant for him to read this—not then, not now—and there was no way in the world he could ask her about it now. It would sound entirely too much like sour grapes. The past was the past, and whatever secrets it held would just have to remain secret for another ten years or more.

After a time, he got up and put the letter in the bottom of the top bureau drawer, covering it up with socks and underwear from his suitcase. Much later, climbing between the crisp-smelling cotton sheets and weighed down by quilts, he managed a smile. Dani, getting married. He resolved to make it top priority to find out all he could about this man who thought he was good enough to be her husband. Bret felt it was a good thing he had come home when he had.

But sleep was a long time coming, and he was beginning to wonder whether it had been a good idea to come home at all.

"GOOD HEAVENS," exclaimed Pauline Westmeyer, examining the scrawl on the back of the boys' bathroom door with an expression of distaste. "Where do kids learn words like this, anyway?"

"What do you expect to find on a bathroom door?" Dani replied. "A love poem? I'll call the janitor."

The two women proceeded down the hall, dodging an occasional overenthusiastic student, who, upon seeing them, immediately pretended to remember the rule about running in the halls—only to forget it again the moment he passed them. Pauline cast Dani a side-long glance. "Speaking of obscenities," she said, "who was that gorgeous fellow you were cuddled up with last night? The one who, I might add, bore no resemblance whatsoever to a certain Todd Renshaw?"

Dani muffled an exclamation of exasperation. Pauline had been teaching at Clayville Elementary almost as long as Dani had, and she could be reasonably counted as one of Dani's best friends. But she had not grown up in Clayville and could, therefore, have no idea of who Bret Underwood was or of the history between Dani and him. Dani wasn't sure whether, in this case, that was a good thing or bad.

"Good heavens," she said, scowling, "the way people talk in this town..." Then, moderating her voice with hard-won patience, she explained, "In the first place, I wasn't cuddling up to anybody. In the second place, he's an old friend. He's staying with my folks for the holidays."

"Is that right...?"

There was an expectant tone to Pauline's murmur, but Dani remained stubbornly silent. She was growing a little irritated with the speculation and innuendo that seemed to be as necessary to her neighbors' survival as the air they breathed. Odd, because usually she found such harmless gossip merely amusing. She reflected wryly that being the target of gossip gave one a whole new perspective on the word *harmless*.

When it became apparent Dani did not intend to elaborate, Pauline prompted, "Well, old friend or not, he's definitely a hunk—to use the vernacular. What does Todd think about this latest development?"

"Nothing yet. I haven't introduced them."

"Are you going to?"

"I guess I'd better," Dani retorted, pushing open the door of her classroom, "before Todd reads about my passionate affair with an out-of-town stranger in his own newspaper!"

Pauline chuckled as she crossed the hall to her own classroom. "Sounds good to me. Nothing like a little scandal to liven up the holidays."

If Dani had been closer, she would have had a pithy reply for that, too. It was perhaps fortunate that Pauline was already out of hearing range.

Dani dumped her books onto her desk and looked skeptically at the withered cactus that sat on the corner of her desk, showing little improvement since yesterday. Not, of course, that she could expect much in a mere sixteen hours, but it did seem that the cactus looked worse this year than it ever had. Maybe she should stop by the library this afternoon and find a book on cacti.

She took a pitcher from the arts-and-crafts cabinet and filled it with water from the girls' bathroom— where, she noticed, there were no unsightly scrawls on the door—and by the time she returned, she was able to put the conversation with Pauline in perspective. She had done enough teasing in her time to be able to take it in good measure from someone else, and there was absolutely no reason why she should be so sensitive on the subject of Bret Underwood. One thing was certain though: she was going to have to get the two men together, and the sooner the better. Maybe tonight, for dinner.

Bret had been sleeping that morning when Dani left for school and her mother absolutely refused to let her wake him. Since her car was still in the school parking lot, Dani had had to accept a ride into town with her father, and she tried to push away the disappointment she felt. It was just that she had counted on having a few moments alone that morning with Bret, and she couldn't shake the feeling that too much had been left unresolved last night.

Certainly, he had not done or said anything to make her feel that way. All in all, the announcement of her almost, not-quiet-certain, possible engagement had gone very well, and Bret had reacted no differently than she had expected; probably not much differently than she herself had reacted when he made the same announcement to her ten years ago. Good humor, goodwill, light banter—those were their trademarks, and Bret had not disappointed her.

Still, she was left *feeling* disappointed and a little uneasy and not quite right about the whole thing in her own mind. Part of it, she supposed, was guilt for not having told Bret before—coupled, of course, with the guilt of enjoying herself with Bret while Todd was working overtime at the paper, and not to even mention the fact that she had not, as of this moment, returned Todd's phone call. But another part was some indefinable feeling that she had let Bret down in some way or he had let her down. She wanted to talk more. She wanted to know what he thought. She wanted his advice.

Which, of course, was ridiculous. What advice could Bret give about a man he didn't even know? What could he possibly say that would be of any value concerning the man she had all but decided she wanted to spend the rest of her life with?

Maybe all she really wanted from Bret was his approval, and looking back over the evening, she realized that for all his easy humor and nonsensical pleasantries, approval was one thing Bret had explicitly not given.

And that, Dani scolded herself as her classroom began to fill, was utterly ridiculous. She was a grown woman and had been delegated the right to make her own decisions for quite some time now. She didn't need Bret Underwood's permission—or approval—to make this, certainly one of the most personal decisions of her life.

But she knew she would never be comfortable until she at least had his opinion.

PAULINE MIGHT HAVE welcomed a scandal to liven up her holidays, but for Dani, the holidays were more than lively enough. The first three hours of the classroom day were spent in diligent application to study, but Dani tried hard to disguise the lessons with so much holiday cheer that the students did not suspect they were actually learning. In social studies, they began a study of Christmas around the world; she passed

out math work sheets that consisted chiefly of ar-
ranging an even number of Christmas ornaments on
the seven branches of a tree, and in English, she assigned a Christmas story to be turned in Friday. After
lunch, she passed out permission slips for the annual
Christmas-tree-cutting field trip, accepted sugges-
tions for the craft projects the children would make for
their parents and—by clever manipulations that only
another teacher could appreciate—persuaded the class
into unanimous agreement on clove-studded oranges
for the mothers and spool tie racks for the dads. During recess, she finally got a chance to call Todd.

"Well," he greeted her, "if it isn't my favorite person. And just in time for my coffee break."

"You know what I don't like about you?" she
challenged him.

"Wait a minute, let me get my list."

"I haven't returned your phone call for almost
twenty-four hours, and you're not even mad."

"Do you know what I don't like about you? I break
a date with you at the last minute, and you're not even
mad."

"Who says I'm not?"

"If you were mad, you wouldn't have returned my
phone call for at least forty-eight hours."

Dani grinned as she leaned back in the creaky swivel
chair and adjusted the blinds so that she could watch
the playground. She was sitting in what was euphe-
mistically called the "teachers' lounge"—in reality
little more than an extension of the janitor's closet
with a desk, a chair and a window—but it afforded a
good view of both the front entrance and the play-

ground. There were three teachers on duty outside, and everything appeared to be as much under control as it could be at recess, so she turned her attention back to the telephone.

"As a matter of fact," she informed Todd blithely, "I would have been more than forty-eight hours' worth of mad, but lucky for you, I was able to get another date at the last minute."

"So I hear."

Dani smothered a groan. "News spreads faster in this town than head colds. Who needs a newspaper?"

"Hey, watch that kind of talk. So who is this combination Greek god and Wall Street genius I'm supposed to be losing you to?"

"Not Wall Street," she corrected. "Lemon Street, California. Why can't anybody understand the difference between *securities* and *security?* It's just Bret— you remember, I told you about him. My old friend from—"

"Sure, I remember. When did he get in?"

"Just yesterday afternoon. It was a real surprise. He didn't let anybody know he was coming. I want you to meet him."

"Sounds great. How about this afternoon? I can knock off early and pick you up after school."

"Can't this afternoon. I start auditions for the school play. Anyway, I was thinking more along the lines of dinner. Seems to me I owe you one somewhere along the line."

"A free meal? Even better. Who's cooking, you or your mom?"

"Don't push your luck, wise guy. My place, seven-thirty."

"I'll be there. What can I bring—besides the main course?"

"I'm warning you—"

"Okay, okay." His voice was smothered with laughter. "I'll bring the wine and a mouthful of compliments on your cooking. Love you."

"Me, too."

Dani hung up the phone, smiling. She didn't know why she had dreaded the call so much; talking with Todd always made her feel good, just as being with him did. Everything about him made her feel good: his smile, his easy humor, his quick grasp of problems and his straightforward approach to them. She really *liked* him, and there weren't very many people anyone could say that about. And why shouldn't she like him? Todd was a great guy; anyone could tell that. Furthermore, anyone could see that she and Todd were perfect for each other. Certainly, Dani had never known anyone with whom she got along better... except, of course, Bret.

And with all of that in mind, there was no reason at all why she should be so ambivalent about marrying Todd Renshaw.

Dani had not exactly had a stellar social life since she'd finished college and settled down for good in Clayville. Part of it was due, of course, to the limits of living in a small town where she knew everybody and everyone knew her and there wasn't much mystery left to lend excitement to romance. Part of it was undoubtedly because of Dani's own high standards. Over the years, she had had casual dates and one or two long-term love affairs, but she had never considered any of them serious.

But from the time she and Todd had started dating, they had been linked in the minds of every onlooker as a couple and for the first time, Dani hadn't minded. Maybe it was because she was getting too old to fight it, maybe it was because everything about her relationship with Todd had seemed to follow the course of least resistance. She had been expecting his marriage proposal since August; by the time he finally made it just before Thanksgiving, she had been more than prepared to say yes. And no one had been more surprised than she was when the words that came out of her mouth were, "I need to think about it, Todd."

Todd took it in good grace, though, of course, he wouldn't have done anything else. He understood that they had both been single for a long time, and there was a lot to think about—finances, living arrangements, careers, children. There were adjustments to be made, and he was willing to give Dani time to get used to the newness of the idea. Deep inside, Dani was sure, he had no doubts as to what her answer would eventually be. Just as she, until yesterday, had had no doubt herself.

Why should Bret's unexpected appearance make any difference?

She didn't know the answer to that, and just thinking about it was threatening to give her a headache. But she knew now she wouldn't be able to make a decision until she talked to Bret.

IF DANI HAD KNOWN HOW much Bret had been counting on those few moments alone with her that morning while he drove her to school, she would have awakened him no matter what her mother said. As it was, with the time-zone change and Bret's restless night, it was after nine o'clock before he awoke, and he was sharply disappointed to find that he had missed her.

There were two reasons he had wanted to get up early. The first was that he still felt he had handled things badly the night before and he wanted a chance to make up for it. The second was that he knew unless he got out of the house early, there would be no way to avoid the years of catching up Dani's parents would insist upon.

Dani's parents were almost as close to him as his own, and he had always enjoyed their company. The two families had been neighbors all their lives and close personal friends, as well. When Bret's father passed away when Bret was nine, Harold Griffin had stepped into the surrogate role as easily as an uncle might have, making the loss much easier for Bret to bear. Holidays had been celebrated around the Griffin table; summer vacations, Labor Day picnics and Sunday dinners had always been joint affairs. Bret had spent as much time at Dani's house as he had at his own, for they were family.

But families entailed certain responsibilities as well as pleasures. Bret didn't mind pitching in to help Anne with the dishes—and he certainly hadn't minded the first hot breakfast he'd had since he'd given up power brunches two years ago. He endured her questions about the state of his health, business and personal life with the same amused tolerance he would have given his own mother, but he didn't object when Harold rescued him just before lunch with the suggestion they take a walk around the place. He enjoyed slipping back into a simpler time with fish stories and tall tales, and there was a basic, uncomplicated pleasure in the sound of their footsteps crunching over icy, stubbly ground, as he listened to the older man's expert comments on everything from the state of the nation to the state of last year's crop. He didn't even mind—not much, anyway—the half a cart of wood he split after lunch; the exercise was good for him. But with one thing and then another, with so much to talk about and so many memories being evoked, he never got around to bringing up the subject of Todd Renshaw, and that was really the only thing on his mind.

It was after three when he finally got away, and he could only hope Dani was still at school. He followed the sound of a slightly out-of-tune piano to the combination cafeteria/auditorium, and that was where he found her.

She was sitting at one of the child-sized gray Formica tables in a child-sized red molded plastic chair, a sheaf of papers spread out before her and a pencil stuck behind her ear. Her attention was on the stage where a dozen or so children were belting out a fair rendition of "Jolly Old St. Nicholas." He stood there for a moment, overwhelmed by that slightly queasy feeling of déjà vu every adult experiences when confronted by a schoolroom situation—as though he should look over his shoulder for the principal before he threw that next spitball—and he wondered why in the world Dani would want to teach in the same school in which she herself had grown up. When viewed like that, she had spent her entire life surrounded by the same four walls. How did she stand it? Convicted criminals served shorter sentences than that.

He moved toward her, glancing dubiously at the undersized chairs before selecting one and sitting down beside her. He wrinkled his nose a little and said under his breath, "Spinach and yeast rolls. The place even smells the same."

Dani's face lit up as she turned to him. "Oh, Bret, good! I was hoping you'd stop by. We're auditioning for the Christmas play. See that little boy with the red hair? I think he'd be perfect for the part of the Mischievous Angel, don't you?"

"Type casting," he replied. And then he grinned. "Remember when old Mrs. Hawkins put on the metronome and made us all skip around the stage to pick the best dancers for her musical production of *The Three Billy Goats*?"

Dani nodded. "Her idea was if you didn't have enough coordination to skip you couldn't be much of a dancer. Good theory. You were the first one out."

"I was the *only* one out," he corrected. "Possibly the only fourth grader in the history of the world who was too clumsy to skip. It was humiliating."

"It was a little cruel, come to think of it."

"I still carry the scars. And you—star of every school play since kindergarten and so graceful you wouldn't trip if somebody tied your shoelaces together—immediately pretended to lose the rhythm so she'd kick you out, too."

"She made me mad."

"You just didn't want me to feel bad."

Dani grinned at him. "We sure had fun, didn't we, drawing scenery backstage while all the other kids were getting yelled at for two hours every afternoon by Mrs. Hawkins just so they could be in her stupid play?"

Bret could still smell the dust of the pastel chalk that had clung to his clothes and hair and dyed his hands blue, but it wasn't that memory that made him smile. It was Dani. "We always had fun," he agreed.

The music stopped, and Dani turned back to the stage. "That was great," she called. "Now, all the girls line up on the right side of the stage—no, Sarah, the right—and all the boys on the left, and get ready to read your lines. Laurie, we'll start with you. Talk real loud now. Pretend your mom's in the back row and you want her to hear you."

"My mom always sits on the front row," Laurie replied smugly.

"Go ahead, Laurie."

Laurie shouted, "Don't cry, little pony! I'm the Christmas Angel and I've come to make all your dreams come true!"

Bret groaned. "This is depressing. Like one of those nightmares when you're back in school again and you discover you've forgotten your algebra book *and* your pants."

Dani arched her eyebrows at him. "I never have nightmares like that. Must be one of those type-A personality things." Then lifting her voice. "That's fine, Laurie. Boys, settle down. Robert, read your line.''

For the next half hour, Bret listened to a dozen or more students alternately shout, mumble and stammer their lines. He entertained himself by waggling his fingers at the pianist—a young sandy-haired woman who kept staring at him and then was continually embarrassed to be caught staring—and by wondering, once again, why Dani had ended up here.

She was good with the children, there was no denying that. She had the patience, the humor and the natural energy it took to work with youngsters, and no doubt she was an excellent teacher. But she also had a great deal more, and in all their childhood plans and dreams, teaching had never even been mentioned as one of Dani's ambitions. Of course, there weren't many options open in a town the size of Clayville for a college-educated woman. He would never understand why she had stayed so long and settled for so little.

When the last little girl reassured the pony and resumed her place among her giggling schoolmates, Dani called out, ''Okay, kids, that was great. I'll be handing out your parts tomorrow morning, and tomorrow afternoon, we'll get together here and start practicing. Does everyone have a ride home?''

To judge by the clamor and excited rush for the door, everyone did. The pianist gathered up her sheet music and came over to them. ''Hi,'' she said, directing herself to Bret. ''I'm Pauline Westmeyer. You must be Dani's friend—''

"Bret Underwood," he supplied, grinning as he got to his feet.

She blushed again. "Sorry for staring. It's just not often that we see an unfamiliar face around here. Are you staying long?"

"I don't know yet."

"He'll be staying," Dani assured her colleague. "I've got enough for him to do to keep him here till Christmas."

"Well, great." Pauline smiled. "I'll be seeing you around, then."

She made a circle of her thumb and forefinger behind her back when she thought Bret couldn't see as she left, and Bret laughed softly.

"Watch it, Hot Stuff," Dani said as she gathered up her papers. "She's divorced and on the prowl, and you're prime pickings."

"I'll consider myself fairly warned." He picked up Dani's attaché case as they started for the exit.

"So, who do you like for the Christmas Angel?"

"The little blond girl," he replied promptly, "in the plaid jumper."

"Type casting," she scoffed. "I'm going to give it to Lisa Carp. She's never played anything more important than a tree, and the part would be good for her confidence."

"Mrs. Hawkins would turn over in her grave. Don't you know the first requirement for being a teacher is to torture the little monsters for everything they're worth?"

Bret pushed open the heavy fire door and they walked into the bright, crisp afternoon.

"How about coming for dinner tonight?"

He glanced at her skeptically. "I don't know. Your mom is making apple dumplings."

"So tell her to send over a few."

"And pork chops."

"I'm making eggplant casserole. Take it or leave it."

"Some choice."

She didn't break stride or alter her tone as she said, "Todd's coming, too."

Bret lifted one eyebrow. "And you want me to chaperone?"

She stopped then and gave him a look he knew too well to ignore. "I want you to be polite, charming and supportive. I mean it, Bret. Best behavior."

"I guess that means I can't eat with my feet on the table."

"Bret . . ."

"Okay, okay. Sounds like an offer I can't refuse." And then he hesitated, squinting a little in the bright winter sunlight. "Listen, Dani," he added, trying not to sound as uncomfortable as he felt, "I guess I was a little insensitive last night. All that joking around when I should've known you wanted me to just shut up and listen. It's just that you caught me off guard, you know? I'm looking forward to meeting your Todd, and I'll be nice to him, even if I hate him. I promise."

The smile that spread across her face was as much in gratitude for what Bret had not said as for what he had. "You won't hate him," she assured him, slipping her arm through his. "And if you do, you don't have to be nice to him. Fair enough?"

He ruffled her hair as he walked her to her car. ''You've got a deal.''

And he hoped Dani wouldn't be too disappointed when it turned out that he did hate Todd Renshaw, because that was exactly what he was fully prepared to do.

Chapter Five

Bret pushed aside the lingerie that was scattered over Dani's bed and stretched out across it on his stomach. "You know," he said, "this is really nice."

He was looking out over the living area from the loft that was Dani's bedroom. When he had last seen the place, it had barely been completed: she had slept on a hammock in the loft, and the only furniture was her grandmother's maple dining room set. The dining set was still there, but it had been joined by a collection of braided scatter rugs, an oversize plush sofa, and several colorful, mismatched chairs and a spinet piano. She had painted the walls a deep Colonial blue with off-white trim and wainscotting. Brass trunks and wrought iron plant stands served as occasional tables, and the built-in shelves her father had designed were crowded with books and collectibles. It was casual, eclectic and fresh; as colorful and energetic as Dani herself, and just as warm. Looking at it, Bret felt the faintest stirrings of envy. She had built a home; all he had was a house.

"All right, what about this?" She came out from behind a country-chintz screen wearing a long, burgundy skirt of some kind of floating, clinging material and a cream-colored sweater with a wide, lace collar.

He turned over to look at her, scrunching a pillow behind his head. "Looks fine." He was careful to keep his voice noncommittal because, of course, she looked more than fine. He was amazed at how fine she looked when she got dressed up, and he was a little puzzled about why he had never noticed it before.

"What about my hair?" She pirouetted toward the mirror, pushing her hair up off her shoulders into a pouf on top. "Up or down?"

He made a face. "Ah, Dani, don't make me do this. Don't you have a girlfriend you can call? What do I know about hair?" She gave him a warning look in the mirror and he relented. "Down. Wear it down. I don't know what the big deal is anyway. You've already hooked the guy, what do you have to impress him for?"

She bent over at the waist, brushing her hair forward. It rippled like exotic silk in the lamplight. "I'm not trying to impress anybody. You're the one who made me change the first dress—"

"It was too tight. I could see your panty line."

"And you're the one who made me snag my only pair of blue stockings—"

"Which wouldn't have happened if you'd worn jeans like I told you to."

She straightened up, caught the whirl of her hair in one hand before it could fall to her shoulders again, and twisted it into a loose knot atop her head. "Why do I get the feeling you'd be just as happy if I served dinner in a chenille bathrobe and bunny slippers? Speaking of dinner, will you run downstairs and put the rolls in?''

''You already did. Jeez, Dani, you'd think you were serving an eight-course dinner for a head of state. What are you so rattled about?''

''I am not rattled,'' she retorted. ''This is the way I always get before a dinner party. I can never remember how to time the vegetables or whether I salted the soup or— Oh!''

''What?''

''My earring's caught! Oh, damn, I hate these earrings, I never wear them—''

''Come here. Stop jerking your head, you're going to hurt yourself.'' He sat up and caught her waist, pulling her back to sit on the bed between his legs. The earring, a dangling contraption of silver wire that greatly resembled a medieval torture device, was snagged in the lace collar of her sweater, and her ineffectual strugglings had only ensnared it further.

''Relax,'' Bret said, working to loosen the delicate lace. Her cinnamon scent drifted up to him, warm and feminine. ''I was a brain surgeon in a former life.''

''You're going to tear my sweater.''

''I'm more concerned about tearing your ear. Stop wiggling.''

''What are you doing with my stocking around your neck?''

Bret glanced disinterestedly at his shoulder, where a dark blue stocking was draped like a scarf. ''That's where you threw it, I guess. Oh-oh.''

''What?'' She sat stiffly, not daring to move.

"The earring's free. My watch is caught."

"Oh, Bret, for heaven's sake!"

"Be still—"

They both froze at the sound of a knock on the door. A second later, the door opened and a man who could only be Todd walked in.

The loft bedroom was perfectly visible from below, and though Bret felt a brief twinge of sympathy for Dani, it did not override the mischievous—and, he had to admit, unworthy—sense of satisfaction he felt for the view Todd must have had. There were the two of them, sitting on the rumpled bed amidst a pile of lingerie in what could very well be mistaken for an embrace; his arms were around Dani and their faces were almost touching as she turned to look at him. Anyone could be forgiven for misinterpreting.

But Todd, seeing them, merely grinned. "Am I early?" he asked.

He set the bottle of wine on the bar and started up the stairs.

"Hurry!" Dani ground out.

For her sake, Bret did and got the watch disentangled just as Todd reached the loft.

Dani leapt to her feet. "Hi, Todd. I want you to meet Bret Underwood. Bret, this is Todd Renshaw."

Bret got to his feet, making a deprecating gesture toward the bed. "I guess you're wondering what's going on."

"With Dani," Todd replied easily, "I've learned not to ask." He extended his hand. "Good to meet you, Bret."

Bret accepted his handshake, but couldn't prevent a puzzled glance at Dani as she plucked her stocking from around his neck. No one, he thought, had the right to be that confident.

Then Dani gasped out, "The rolls!" and pushed past them. "Come downstairs," she called over her shoulder. "Make yourselves at home. Somebody pour the wine."

Todd grinned at Bret. "Great little hostess."

Bret got the glasses while Todd opened the wine. Dani kept herself busier than she probably needed to be in the kitchen in order, Bret suspected, to give the two men time alone together. That was not necessarily a good idea.

Bret guessed Todd was probably close to Dani's age, around Bret's own height and—he had to reluctantly admit—looked to be in pretty good shape for a newspaper man. He wore tortoiseshell glasses, a tweed jacket and a sweater vest over an Oxford shirt. He had probably, Bret reflected, been a nerd in high school, the kind of guy Dani wouldn't have looked at twice. But then, none of them was in high school anymore.

"So, Bret," Todd said, handing him a glass of wine, "tell me about yourself."

"I think that's supposed to be my line."

"I anticipated as much," Todd replied, and reached into his coat pocket for a folded sheet of paper, "and thought I'd save us both some time."

Bret glanced at the paper Todd handed him and had to fight back a grin. It was a typed résumé, complete with salary, family history, career goals and golf handicap. "I see Dani's dad has already given you the third degree."

"After the second date," Todd admitted.

They walked back toward the living area. "Did you pass?"

"The jury's still out."

Bret chuckled. "The Griffins aren't known for making hasty decisions."

"That's okay. I'm a patient man."

Bret did not imagine the underlying meaning behind those words—it was not a warning, merely a statement of fact. He turned to add another log to the fire he had built earlier, and when Todd took the big, comfortably worn chair by the fireplace, it was with the natural ease of a man who had sat there many times before. Bret sat on the hearth.

There wasn't much room, and Bret accidentally upset one of Dani's collection of bells when he straightened out his legs. There must have been a hundred of them, arranged along the mantel, grouped on the hearth and on the two small shelves flanking it—sleigh bells, doorbells, hand bells, glass bells, silver, gold and copper bells. Bret wondered how she ever found time to keep them all dusted.

He righted the small clapper bell he had overturned, murmuring, "'Bells, bells, bells, bells...'"

"'The tintinnabulation of the bells,'" Todd finished, and Bret looked at him sharply.

"Bret started me collecting them," Dani said, coming into the room with a plate of hors d'oeuvres. She diplomatically chose to sit on a cushion on the floor between the two men and first offered the plate to Todd.

"Don't put that on me," Bret objected. "That's one vice you developed all on your own."

"You were into bells?" inquired Todd.

"He was into cows." Dani thrust the hors d'oeuvres platter into Bret's hand and stood up, lifting a rust-scarred cowbell from its place on the mantel. "Bret gave me this when I was five. It was the first present a boy ever gave me."

"You were easily impressed," Bret admitted. "Why do you keep that filthy thing? It ruins your whole decor."

She made a face at him, and Todd reached for the bell. "Who did the artwork on the side?" he asked. He turned the bell to face them, clearly showing the crooked letters carved into the tin: BU + DG.

"Dani did," Bret said.

"Bret did," Dani answered at the same time. Then they looked at each other and laughed.

"Who knows?" Bret shrugged. "That was over twenty years ago. God, I never thought I'd be old enough to say that."

"Did any of us?" Dani took the cowbell and replaced it carefully on the mantel, then resumed her place on the floor, smiling at him.

Bret resisted the impulse to slip his arm around her shoulders in a friendly hug and contented himself with smiling back at her. It was a good moment, and even Todd's presence couldn't spoil it.

Bret was amazed, as a matter of fact, at how little Todd's presence did to spoil any part of the evening.

He kept waiting for the other man to do something or say something to irritate him, but Todd never did. Either Todd Renshaw was incredibly well rehearsed, or he was really pleasant company. The fact that Bret couldn't find anything wrong with Todd was, in truth, the only thing that annoyed him.

They talked about the changes that had occurred in Clayville since Bret's last visit, and Todd was able to put personal stories into a social and economic context in a way that formed a fascinating picture. Bret asked about real-estate prices and discovered Todd knew more off the top of his head than Bret's expensive L.A. firm had uncovered in a month of research. Eventually, the talk turned to Bret's business and Bret learned Todd knew a great deal more about the psychology of crime than he did. In fact, Todd knew more about almost everything than he did, and it was easy to see why Dani liked him. Bret should have resented that, but he was too interested in the other man's conversation to pause for reflection.

He watched Dani and Todd carefully, trying to read between the lines into the nature of their relationship, but that, too, proved futile. There were no lingering touches, no secret glances. That could indicate a couple so secure in their relationship, they had grown past the need for open displays of affection. It could mean they were simply being polite for Bret's sake. Or it could mean . . . nothing.

Bret only knew if he had a girl who looked as good as Dani did that night, he would have been hard put to keep his hands off her. Maybe Todd was used to it, but Bret's eyes were continually drawn back to Dani in amazed appreciation at the way the soft sweater outlined her figure and the way the skirt alternately floated and clung when she moved; the way her eyes sparkled when she laughed and the way soft tendrils from her upswept hair escaped to frame her face. When had she gotten so grown-up, so feminine? Did Todd have any idea how lucky he was?

The only awkward moment came at the end of the evening, when neither man could decide who was supposed to leave first. Though it would have been against his better judgment, Bret would have accepted a signal from Dani if she had wanted to end the evening alone with Todd. He knew her well enough to realize that the point of the meeting would not be served until she and he had a chance to talk about it, so he made no move to go. And when Todd finally glanced at his watch with a rueful expression and made some comment about the time, Bret knew he had read Dani correctly. She walked Todd to the door, and though Bret should have been ashamed of himself, he made sure that he could see them at all times. Todd, observing this, kissed Dani on the cheek and waved good-night to Bret.

Bret had to admit that any man who could take that kind of treatment in such good humor deserved a Good Sport of the Year award at the very least.

"So." Dani leaned against the door, her cheeks flushed and her eyes bright with expectation. "What do you think?"

Bret lounged back on the sofa and swung his feet onto the brass trunk in front of it. "I think he's charming. Another hour, and we'd probably be picking out a china pattern together.''

"Be serious."

"I am serious. He's a great guy."

Bret patted the place beside him on the sofa, but Dani was too keyed up to sit. She began gathering up coffee cups and cocktail napkins.

"I knew you'd like him. Do you think he's good-looking?"

"Not my type."

"Well, I do. I like that swarthy, intellectual look."

"He's not swarthy. And his nose is too big."

Dani glanced at Bret critically. "Well, maybe he's not as good-looking as you—"

"Am I?" Bret pretended to preen.

"But I think he's got interesting looks. Character."

"And I don't?"

She took the coffee cups to the sink. "You're too blond, too tan, too perfect."

"Don't forget built."

She returned, wiping her hands on a dish towel, and looked at him assessingly. "You're too...Hollywood. You need a flaw."

"I've got plenty of them. You just can't see them because you adore me so much." He reached for her hand and pulled her down beside him. "What is this, anyway, a beauty contest? Your Todd's a nice guy, and looks aren't everything. What's really on your mind?"

She tossed the dish towel aside and sighed as she leaned her head back against his shoulder. "You know that."

"Yeah, I do. But I want to hear you say it."

"Oh, Bret. Marriage..." She twisted her head around to look at him, uncertainty in her eyes. "What's it like?"

He chuckled. "I'm the last person you should ask about that."

"But at least you did it," she insisted. "Why?"

"Oh, honey, I don't know." Absently, his hand caressed her shoulder. "Looking back, I really don't know."

And then something struck him. *If you knew, it might make a difference.* Maybe that was the key. If he had known, back then, about this other person who loved him, it *would* have made a difference, and it shouldn't have. Not if the marriage was right, not if the love was real....

That was something he had never realized before, and it disturbed him. There was something there he needed to think about, but he was aware that Dani's expression had become puzzled, so he added thoughtfully, "I'll tell you one thing. If I had it to do over again, I wouldn't marry in the heat of passion. I mean, there should be that, but it takes more, I think. A lot more."

"Like what?"

"I've got a better question for you. Why didn't you ever do it before?"

"Get married?" She shrugged and settled back against his shoulder again, curling her legs beside her on the sofa. "I don't know, lots of reasons. It took me so long to get a place of my own—well, almost a place of my own—and I guess I had to fight so hard to show my independence, it became sort of a habit. And I never found anybody I liked well enough to settle down with—or anyone who could put up with me for more than a few months. The time just never seemed right."

"And now?"

She hesitated, but only for a minute. "I'm thirty-three years old," she said. "I'm tired of living alone. I want to care about someone and know someone cares about me. I want to build a future with somebody, maybe have children, and that kind of thing can't wait forever. I don't want to grow old alone."

Bret ruffled her hair. "Hell of a reason, kid."

"And I love Todd," she added. "I really do. He's easy to talk to. We get along great. Everybody says we make a perfect couple."

"It's looking better and better."

She sighed again. "I know how that sounds. I couldn't talk like this to anyone but you. I mean, everyone expects you to just go into raptures about the man you're going to marry, but you have to be practical. You have to think about these things. Like you said, there should be more than passion."

"But a little passion never hurt."

"I never said I wasn't passionate," she objected. "I just don't let it go to my head."

"And nothing scares Dani Griffin more than change."

"Right," she admitted.

A silence fell and Bret wished he knew what to say. He wished he knew what Dani *wanted* him to say. The whole situation would have been a great deal easier if only he had been able to find something wrong with

Todd, and he hadn't realized until that moment how much he had counted on disliking the man.

He gave her shoulders a reassuring squeeze and lowered his chin to rest atop her hair. She smelled wonderful. The sweater was as silky as kitten fur against his fingers, and the shape of her arm beneath it was soft and feminine. He had never noticed before how well they fit together, her head coming just beneath his chin, her hip resting naturally against the curve of his. How good it felt to sit with her like this, holding her.

"You know," he said after a moment, "I didn't expect any of this when I came home. It seems like all my life, you're the one thing that never changed. The one thing I could always count on."

"Maybe that's not a good thing."

Without his realizing it, his arm had drifted down, encircling her, his hand resting lightly on her rib cage. He could feel the delicate pulse of her heart just beneath her left breast. An awareness went through him that started as a tingling in his fingers and spread to a warmth that tightened his muscles. The reaction shouldn't have surprised him: she was a beautiful woman, soft and feminine, and she was lying in his arms. But she was Dani.

His voice was a little thick as he replied, "I don't think I'm the one you should be asking about this."

She turned to look at him. Her eyes were a silvery, candlelit shade, and so close that, had she been anyone else, he would have closed them with a kiss. And there was something in those eyes... something that caught him off guard and made his heart beat a little faster, almost as though she knew what he was thinking. And she didn't mind.

She said softly, "You're the only one I can ask, Bret."

He could feel the faint stirring of her breath on his cheek and the silken brush of her hair tickling his throat. Her scent tantalized him, making him wonder if traces of it lingered on her skin and what it would be like to taste. They were fleeting thoughts, ephemeral feelings that would hardly bear close examination, not even with that open, almost expectant look in Dani's eyes all but urging him to do so.

His throat felt a little dry as he swallowed, and he straightened up, forcing a smile. "Tell you what, then," he said. "Better let me think about it awhile."

He kissed her on the forehead and stood up. "Meanwhile, don't do anything rash."

"Who, me?"

She walked with him to the door, her arm looped around his waist. "Thanks for coming, Bret."

"Have you ever known me to refuse a free meal?"

"No, I mean…" She stopped and looked up at him, resting her hand lightly on his chest. "Thanks for coming home when you did. You always know, don't you?"

"*We* always know," he corrected gently.

She smiled. "And thanks for being nice tonight. Even if you didn't want to."

"I did outdo myself, didn't I?"

"You're amazing when you apply yourself."

He opened the door and they stood for a moment in the cold draft of night air. "I knew you'd like Todd," she told him. She leaned forward and brushed his lips lightly with a kiss. "He's a lot like you. Good night, Bret."

The scent of cinnamon and vanilla lingered on Bret's skin through the crisp walk home and followed him into his dreams.

Chapter Six

"What kind of perfume does Dani wear?" Bret asked Anne the next morning.

Her eyes twinkled as she glanced over her shoulder at him. "Christmas shopping, are you?"

She bent to take a pan of muffins out of the oven—blueberry, from the smell of them—and Bret was glad she missed the look of discomfiture that came over his face. He didn't know where the question had come from, except that it had been on his mind all night, and now that the words were out, they almost seemed too personal.

Besides, he hadn't given the first thought to what to give Dani for Christmas.

"Do you know," Anne said, a little frown playing with her brow as she straightened up with the muffin tin, "I don't believe Dani ever wears perfume. Aunt Ida sends her a bottle of toilet water every year, and every year it ends up in the box for the poor. But I'll try to find out if there's any particular fragrance she likes, if you want."

"No, I guess not." Bret made his voice casual as he took a bowl from the counter and helped himself to the oatmeal that was simmering in the big kettle on the stove. "Perfume's not the right kind of gift for Dani, anyway. I was just trying to think of something girlie."

Anne laughed. "You have been away a long time! Her father and I are trying to decide between a pair of snowshoes and a new bobsled. 'Girlie' has never been her style."

"Maybe she'd like a new puppy," Bret teased.

"Don't you dare!" Anne set the basket of muffins on the table and gave him a sidelong glance. "Of course, this year, she might be easier to buy for. China and silver should be high on the list. How did dinner go last night?"

Bret brought the coffeepot to the table. "Not too bad. She didn't burn anything."

"You know that's not what I mean."

Bret sat down with his bowl of oatmeal, choosing his words carefully. "Her new fella is a nice guy."

Anne sat next to him, buttering a muffin. "We think so, too."

"Miss Annie," Bret said abruptly, "could I ask you something?"

"Of course, dear."

"Do you remember when I got married?"

Her eyes twinkled again as she bit into the muffin, reminding Bret very much of her daughter. "Why, yes, now that you mention it, I do vaguely recall something of the sort. Why do you ask?"

Bret kept his eyes on the cup of coffee he was pouring. "I just wondered if you remembered how Dani felt about the whole thing at the time."

Anne's attention seemed to quicken, and Bret wondered if he had revealed too much—and then he wondered why he thought he had anything to hide from Anne Griffin in the first place.

"I'm not sure I know what you mean," she said.

He pushed the coffee cup across the table to her and poured another for himself. "I mean..." And he looked at Anne. "Dani never liked Laura, did she?"

Anne seemed to hesitate, and then she smiled, almost apologetically. "Bret, you know how it is with you two. You're the only brother Dani's ever had, and all her life, she's worshiped the ground you walk on. If she didn't like your wife, it was only because she didn't get to pick her out herself."

"She never told me," Bret said slowly. He was thinking of the letter that was hidden upstairs in his underwear drawer. After last night, he had promised himself he'd forget about it. Now, he supposed he should've thrown it away, because it was obvious he would never be able to forget about it.

Anne smiled at him over the rim of her cup. "Would it have mattered?"

Bret hesitated and then reached for the milk pitcher, pouring a little over his oatmeal. "Yeah," he admitted. "I think it would. If I had known...I might have thought twice."

"And now you resent Dani for not saving you from a painful divorce."

Bret looked at Anne in surprise. Resent Dani? A protest formed on his lips but died unspoken. Because now that Anne had said it, he realized that it *was* resentment he had been feeling, ever since he read that letter. Deeply buried and carefully disguised, but, yes, resentment. Anger, as much as he tried to deny it, because of all the times in their lives, why did she have to pick that one to keep the truth from him? *It could have made a difference, damn it.* And though he was ashamed of himself, he couldn't help it. Dani had cheated him of the most important thing she had to give—her honesty. How could he not resent that?

He tried to smile as he glanced down at the cooling oatmeal. "After all these years, I guess I'm still looking for someone to blame. Stupid, isn't it?"

Anne said sympathetically, "I know it was hard on you, Bret."

"They say it's harder on the woman, but I don't see how that can be."

And again he hesitated, looking for the right words, shaking his head a little when they wouldn't come. "Don't misunderstand me, it wasn't that I was still in love with her when we broke up. It's just that, growing up like I did, with my folks and you, I expected marriage to last forever. There just wasn't any question in my mind that was the way it was supposed to be. It was hard to adjust to—I don't know, losing an illusion. Facing up to the fact that I had invested so much of myself—so much of my expectations—in what turned out to be a temporary arrangement. Do you understand what I mean?"

"Of course, I do. But it's not always an illusion, Bret, and it's not supposed to be temporary. I'd be very disappointed in you if you turned out to be a cynic."

"Not a cynic," he told her, lifting his spoon again. "Just cautious. And a little scared. I think Dani wants me to tell her whether or not to marry Todd," he confessed suddenly.

"Ah." She nodded, sipping her coffee. "And now the shoe's on the other foot."

"I guess it is."

"You're afraid she'll do what you tell her."

"Or she won't."

"No, she probably will. Or she'll at least think about it."

A rueful smile touched Bret's lips as he heard his own words repeated back to him. "And I don't want that responsibility."

She smiled at him.

"All right," he admitted, turning back to the oatmeal again. "I guess I understand where she was coming from all those years ago. But it doesn't make it any easier." In fact, it made it harder. He knew the end of his own story, but who could tell the end of Dani's? He didn't want her to hate him in ten years for what he hadn't said, any more than for what he had.

"Just out of curiosity," Anne said casually, "what would you tell her?"

And that was the hard part. He liked Todd. Dani liked Todd. The two of them seemed perfect for each other. If he were any kind of friend, he would tell her not to be a fool, to grab the guy before he got away and have a great life. So why was he holding back? Why was there any doubt in his mind at all? Marriage was more than a change in life-style, it was a lifetime commitment, and he still believed that despite his own failure. Marriage was a sacrament, a huge, soul-altering progression. Was it the shadow of his own mistake that stood in the way? Or was it that he was afraid Dani would take his advice?

The back door opened with a gust of cold air and Harold came in, his cheeks ruddy from the outdoor temperatures, his eyes twinkling like a good-natured Santa. "I've got the tractor hooked up," he announced, rubbing his hands. "Is everybody ready?"

"What are you doing, going out in that cold without your breakfast?" Anne scolded. She got to her feet to help her husband off with his jacket. "I told you, we've got plenty of time before they get here."

Bret was grateful for the reprieve from disturbing thoughts. "Before who gets here?" he asked. "Where are you going?"

"We," corrected Anne, hanging her husband's jacket on a hook by the door. "It's a family affair, always has been, always will be, though heaven knows how it ever got started."

"Don't be a Scrooge, young lady," Harold said, pinching his wife's cheek. "You know you love it."

"As if I didn't have enough to do around here," Anne pretended to complain, but her smile gave her away.

"Annual Christmas-tree expedition," Harold explained to Bret as he filled his coffee cup. "I'm sure Dani mentioned it to you. She reminded me only this morning to get out an extra jacket for you."

"No, she didn't mention it. She never tells me anything." But it didn't sound too bad, tromping through the woods in search of a tree. It might even be fun. Of course, it would be a lot more fun if Dani were along. "I'm surprised she didn't want to come," he added, sipping his coffee. "It's not like Dani, leaving something as important as a Christmas tree in somebody else's hands."

"Oh, she'll be here," Anne assured him.

"But it's a school day," Bret pointed out.

Harold's eyes twinkled as he sat down and buttered a muffin. "Exactly."

THE BRIGHT YELLOW SCHOOL bus that pulled up in front of the Griffin house forty-five minutes later disgorged twenty chattering, laughing, hyperkinetic eight-year-olds. Dani stood on the bus steps, calling out instructions and admonitions while Anne and Harold greeted the children and tried to arrange them in some semblance of order. Bret stood a little to the side, looking confused and somewhat overwhelmed.

"All right," Dani called, clapping her hands for attention. "All right, you know the rules. Has everyone got his partner?"

There was a great deal of scrambling around, squealing and coattail pulling, followed by a chorus of "I do!" and "Here she is!" and "Miss Griffin, tell Tammy to stop holding my hand!"

Dani waited until they had quieted down. "Remember, stay ten feet behind the tractor. And what happens to anyone who runs or leaves the group?"

The consensus was that the offender would have to go back to the house or wait in the bus or something equally unpleasant.

"Jason, give Mr. Griffin the trees."

A proud little boy walked over to the wagon that was attached to the tractor and presented Harold with a flat of seedling pines. Harold made an appropriate fuss over them before settling them securely against the bed of the wagon. He then climbed onboard the tractor, started the ignition and raised his hand. "Wagons, ho!" he shouted.

The children loved that, and fell into place a safe distance behind the wagon as the tractor chugged down the path that led toward the woods at the back of the house.

Anne took up her place on the left flank of the group, and Dani fell behind, waving to Bret to join her. "Surprise," she said, her eyes sparkling as he came up to her. "Sorry I forgot to mention this last night, but I knew you wouldn't want to miss it."

"You didn't forget. You just knew if you warned me, I'd be sure to sleep late."

She gave him a playful punch in the ribs. "And I'd be sure to wake you up."

Bret looked wonderful today in one of her father's plaid flannel jackets, jeans and borrowed work boots. His hair was tousled and seemed to pick up sun highlights even through the dull, overcast sky, and his skin was roughened and weather chapped. Already, he had begun to lose that polished California boy look, and was beginning to resemble the Bret she had once known.

"So, now that I've been recruited," he said, "what am I supposed to do?"

"Just keep your eyes open—for trees and kids."

"I don't know. Twenty kids and four adults— there's something wrong with those odds."

She laughed. "Coward."

"Where are we going, anyway?"

"Where we always go. That pine meadow at the back of your place."

He repeated blankly, "My place?"

"You don't mind, do you?" she teased him. "Should we be paying you a finder's fee?"

He shook his head, looking a little distracted. "No, it's just that it sounded funny when you said that...my place. I'm not used to thinking of it like that."

"How do you think of it?" she asked curiously.

He hesitated, then shrugged. "The property, mostly. Or sometimes my folks' place. Not mine."

It struck Dani suddenly that there was something sad about that, almost lonely. Bret had deliberately distanced himself from what was rightfully his, he had practically made himself a self-proclaimed orphan, and she would never understand why. She wondered if even he did.

She wanted to slip her arm around him in a gesture of comfort, but wasn't sure how that would look to the children. There was no chance to pursue the subject further because just then Tommy Anderson hit Kathy Sewell and it was clear this expedition was not going to leave much time for socializing.

Dani was amazed and amused at how, after an initial awkwardness and pretended reluctance, Bret stepped in to help with the children as naturally as though he had spent half his life surrounded by noisy eight-year-olds. Dani had observed that it took most people, particularly unmarried men, some time to adjust to being around children, to try to find an attitude toward them with which they were comfortable. Bret didn't have that problem; he simply treated them as he would any other perfectly capable, reasoning human beings. Within twenty minutes, half the girls had a crush on him and the boys were hanging on his every word.

"Do you know something?" Dani commented when she caught up with him again. "I think you'd make a good daddy."

"No, I wouldn't."

"Why not?"

His eyes twinkled as he replied, deadpan, "Because I don't like kids."

"Oh, right." She smothered a grin. "Doesn't exactly fit in with your Hollywood image, does it?"

"Right." Then he lifted his face, grimacing a little as a flake of snow drifted down. "And neither does thrashing through the woods in the middle of a snowstorm."

Dani laughed and slipped her arm through his. "*I* think it's romantic," she declared. "I hope it snows and snows!"

Bret smiled down at her, and there was a tenderness in his eyes, a simple, unabashed pleasure at her touch, that made her feel warm all over. And then she was embarrassed because *romantic* was not what she had meant to say at all, but when he looked at her like that, she almost wished that he was someone different, or that she was, and that romance was what they both had on their minds . . . she didn't know what she wished.

It was a confusing, tangled train of thought that made her look away from him uncomfortably, and she was glad that she did not have the opportunity to pursue it further. Just then, the children noticed the snow and an excited clamor grew up. Dani dropped Bret's arm and moved forward, leading the children in a rollicking rendition of "Frosty the Snowman."

The snow was not heavy, nor was there enough accumulation to do more than dust the tops of the tall grasses and frost the branches of the pines. A gentle mist of white, however, was all that was needed to add authenticity to the search for the perfect tree, and Dani didn't care what Bret said: it *was* romantic. The entire day was. This time with the children in the woods was always her favorite field trip of the year, and having Bret here made it twice as special—almost magical. Having Bret here made *her* feel like a child again with the entire world laid open at her feet, full of possibilities and bursting with promise. Having Bret here made everything seem right again, and she had not felt that sense of rightness since . . . since the last time he had been here. She realized with a sudden pang how much he had taken out of her life when he went away. And how unfair it was that he couldn't stay.

Harold was an absolute wizard when it came to children, and managed—by some method Dani never could figure out—to get them all to agree enthusiastically on the perfect tree, which also happened to be one he had marked weeks ago for that very purpose. He took saw in hand and everyone cheered and applauded as the small tree fell, then Bret helped him load it into the wagon.

"Well, that's that," Bret declared, rubbing the pine sap off his hands. "One less unsightly pine cluttering up the forest. Let's get out of here before all these little darlings catch cold."

Dani laughed. "What a wimp! It must be all that California wine in your blood. We're not even half-finished yet. We've got two more trees to cut—one for my folks, and one for me."

Bret groaned and shivered elaborately. "I should've known. Nothing's ever easy with you in charge."

Two more trees fell to the blade of the hand saw, both were loaded safely onto the wagon, and then as Anne spread out a picnic of hot chocolate and sandwiches on the tail board of the wagon, the tree-planting ceremony began.

Each year, a boy and a girl were chosen to do the honors, and this year Jimmy Skinner and Amy Carney had been elected. Amy carried the little box of saplings proudly, but Jimmy complained, "How come we have to plant trees, anyway? There's nothing but trees everywhere you look. My daddy says you can't grow rocks out here for the trees."

Bret, who had taken the shovel from Harold to dig the six small holes, paused and grinned. But Dani explained patiently, "We always give back what we take from the land, Jimmy. You know that."

"But we only took three trees," Jimmy pointed out. "How come we have to plant six?"

"The other three trees are our Christmas gift to Mother Nature."

"I don't know what you're complaining about," Bret said. "You don't have to dig the holes. Come over here and give me a hand."

Jimmy pretended to be put out, but Dani could tell he was secretly pleased at being given a man's job. And Bret stepped back to let him do it, despite the fact that the holes were already deep enough for planting.

"I don't know why we have to put 'em way over here, anyway," said Jimmy, grunting a little as he dug the tip of the shovel into the frozen soil. "We should've put 'em near the creek, where the digging's easier."

Bret raised his eyebrows, but replied, "There are too many big oaks near the creek. They'd choke out the seedlings."

"Don't matter." Jimmy turned over another spade tip full of earth. "They're gonna freeze, anyhow."

Bret moved over to Dani and murmured, "Smart kid. I'd say he's got the makings of a farmer."

She shrugged and stuffed her hands into the pockets of her parka. "Seedlings are cheap, and replanting is a good habit for the kids to get into. Besides, some of them do make it through the winter—which is why we always plant more than we need. You'd be surprised."

Bret nodded toward the boy. "Who is he?"

"That's Jimmy Skinner," Dani replied. "I guess he did pick up a few things about farming from his father—like how hard this land is to work. Your dad always did say if there was a profit to be made in rocks and pines, he'd be rich."

Bret nodded absently, and Dani noticed that a shadow had fallen over his face.

"What?" she inquired, looking at him closely.

"Nothing." He glanced back at her. "You just re-minded me of two unpleasant things I have to do. Call my office and go talk to Skinner. Will you come with me?"

"Do you mean now?"

"No, but maybe this weekend."

"Sure. I can understand why you wouldn't be looking forward to kicking your tenant out...." He scowled at her and she ignored him. "But why is call-ing your office so unpleasant?"

He looked surprised as he considered the question. "Maybe because I'm having so much fun freezing my butt off out here with you, I can hardly bear the thought of all that dreary sunshine I left behind?"

"Or maybe," she suggested, unable to keep from pushing just a little, "you're just beginning to realize what you really left behind here a long time ago."

Bret looked at her for a moment, and though his expression was unreadable, it made her heart beat just a little faster and for no reason whatsoever. And then he turned back to Jimmy.

"All right, friend," he called, "that looks deep enough." He went over to Amy, who stood ready with the box of seedlings. "Young lady, will you do the honors?"

DANI DISTRIBUTED peanut-butter-and-jelly sand-wiches, paper cups of hot chocolate and homemade cookies, and Anne spread blankets and cushions beneath the shelter of the trees for the children to sit on. When everyone was settled down, they begged Dani for The Story, as they always did. Somehow, through the magic grapevine of childhood, rumors of The Story were passed down from generation to generation, so that every class was just as eager to hear it as the one before.

Dani brushed a light film of snow off a rock and sat down, cuddling a cup of chocolate with her gloved hands. Her eyes twinkled as she pretended to protest, "Oh, it's a dull story. You don't want to hear it."

"I want to hear about the bear!"

"I want to hear about the Indians!"

"But it's history," Dani insisted with a dismissing wave of her hand. "You don't want to hear about history when we're not in school."

"Tell us about the bear!"

Bret sat beside her on the rock, grinning. "Yeah, tell us about the bear."

Dani smiled and scooted over to make room for him, deliberately prolonging the suspense by drinking from her cup. Then she said, "Well, all right. But you have to be very quiet and still, and no throwing food."

"We will!"

"We won't!"

Twenty pairs of eyes turned expectantly on her as she began. "A long, long time ago, a man and a woman called Hannah and Zaccariah came all the way from Pennsylvania in a covered wagon."

"Like that wagon?" interrupted Billy Sims, pointing to the wagon that held the Christmas trees.

The other children shushed him, but Dani nodded. "A lot like that, except they put a roof on it with wire and canvas to keep the rain and wind out. Those kinds of wagons were called prairie schooners because, when a whole bunch of them moved through the tall grass on the prairie, they looked just like boats on the ocean, and *schooner* is another name for a boat. Now Hannah and Zac—we'll call him that for short—they came out here all by themselves, because that was in the time before many people knew about the good farm land out here, and they wanted to be the first to get here and start growing wheat and corn. And so they were. This whole state—" she made a wide sweeping gesture with her arm "—was big and empty, so empty, you can hardly imagine it, and hardly anybody lived here except prairie dogs and a few buffalo and bears . . . and Indians."

The snow made a tinkling sound as it struck the tops of the trees, but beneath their branches the children were dry and protected from the wind. Harold and Anne leaned back against the wagon with their arms around each other's waists, watching the scene benevolently. Bret sat close to Dani, munching a handful of cookies and sipping chocolate, keeping her warm. The children listened expectantly.

"Well," Dani went on, "they got here just about this time of year. It was cold, and snowing a lot harder than it is now. And it so happened that Hannah, Zac's wife, was going to have a baby—"

"And there was no room for her in the inn," piped up Tiffany Wales, and Dani smiled at her.

"There weren't even any inns," she said. "So you know what they had to do? They had to make a tent from the canvas that came off their wagon to live in until Zac could cut down enough trees to build a house. And they built their tent right over there—" she raised her arm and all eyes followed "—underneath that big oak tree.

"But first," she went on, "they had to find something to eat. They had used up most of their food coming out here, and Hannah didn't have anything left in her barrels except a handful of coffee, a scoop of flour, and a few beans. So all day, Zac would go off hunting while Hannah stayed here by the tent, chopping down branches to prop up against the tent to keep the wind out. How would you like to camp out here in the woods in the middle of the winter?"

Several boys volunteered enthusiastically that they'd like it just fine, but Dani assured them, "It was cold. And they were hungry. Do you know why?"

"Because old Zac wasn't much of a shot," murmured Bret, and Dani shot him a warning look.

"Because they used up all their beans," said one little girl.

"Because the animals were hiding," suggested another.

"That's right," Dani said. "It's winter, and you don't see many animals running around, do you? The smart ones are up in their nests, staying warm. So poor Zac and Hannah used up the last of their provisions, and they thought they were going to starve. Zac kept going out every day, looking for game, but he was getting weaker and weaker. Pretty soon, he wouldn't be able to hunt at all.

"And then one morning..." Dani paused for dramatic emphasis, her eyes sweeping the assembly. "Hannah got up and pushed back the flap of the tent and looked out. And there, right at her doorstep, was a haunch of venison, all ready to be cooked. And leading away from the meat were footprints in the snow."

"Indian footprints!"

"Bear footprints!"

Dani smothered a smile and went on. "That venison saved their lives. With something to eat, Zac got stronger and was able to hunt again. But they kept wondering—who had brought it to them? They were all alone here. Who had left the footprints in the snow?"

"A ghost," someone whispered.

"A spaceship man," suggested someone else.

"One day," Dani went on, "Zac managed to shoot a couple of squirrels. And you know what he did? He took one of them and tied it to a low branch of the oak tree. And the next morning, it was gone, with nothing left but footprints in the snow."

There were murmurs of awe among the children. Dani loved it.

"And so it went all winter," she continued. "Whenever Zac and Hannah thought they were surely going to starve, there would be a squirrel or a rabbit or a pile of winter berries left on their doorstep. And whenever Zac had a little luck at hunting, he would leave half of whatever he caught tied to the old oak tree for their mysterious visitor. And that way, they survived the winter.

"Then the snow began to thaw, and it was almost time for Hannah's baby to come. One day while Zac was out cutting trees, Hannah went down to the creek for water..."

"Long walk," commented Jimmy Skinner skeptically.

"Yes, it was," agreed Dani. "But people didn't have electric water pumps back then, and the only way to get water was to draw it from the creek with a bucket."

"Should've pitched their tent closer," Jimmy said.

The other children looked irritated, anxious to get on with the story, but Dani explained patiently, "If they had done that, the creek might have flooded when the snow melted and washed them both away."

Jimmy looked satisfied, and Dani continued with the story. "While Hannah was bent over, dipping the bucket in the water, she heard a rustling noise behind her. She looked up and—"

"A bear!"

"An Indian!"

"It was the biggest, meanest, *hungriest* looking bear you ever saw. This bear had been hibernating all winter, you know, and Hannah must have looked like she would make a pretty good breakfast, because he reared up on his hind legs—and when he did, he was almost twice as big as Hannah—and he let out a roar that shook the treetops, and he started charging toward her."

Her audience was spellbound, and Dani played it for all it was worth. "Poor Hannah. She screamed as loud as she could. She threw the water bucket at the bear, but it just bounced right off him, he didn't even seem to feel it. He just kept on coming. She tried to scramble up the bank and run away, but she fell down, and when she looked up, there was that bear still coming toward her. He was almost on her, with his big, yellow teeth gleaming, and his black claws stretched out... and all of a sudden, the bear stopped and fell down dead.

"Now, Zac had heard his wife scream, and about that time, he came bursting through the bushes with his shotgun in his hand, and he saw Hannah lying there on the ground where she had fallen. He ran over toward her and just about reached her when he heard a noise and he spun around. He was face-to-face with—" Dani paused for effect. "An Indian! And, oh, was this Indian a fearsome sight! His hair was all shaved off except for one long strip down the middle, and he had designs painted all over his face and feathers dangling in his ears and animal skins around his neck. He just stood there, frowning at Zac and looking as fierce and mean as the devil himself. Zac thought for sure both he and Hannah were goners, and he was so scared that when he lifted his gun and tried to aim, he couldn't even pull the trigger because his hands were shaking so badly."

Her audience was rapt, and Dani lowered her voice, leaning toward them a little as they leaned toward her. "Zac got the Indian in his sights. He put his finger on the trigger. He started to squeeze it. And then.... And then he noticed the bow in the Indian's hand, and the bear lying dead with an arrow through its heart. And he knew he'd almost made the biggest mistake of his life. He had almost shot the man who had kept them alive through the winter. The man who had left the footprints in the snow.

"The Indian's name was Walks-Among-Trees. Funny name, isn't it? But it sounded a lot prettier in Indian language. Walks-Among-Trees went home with Hannah and Zac, and that night, Hannah's baby was born. They named him Walker, after their new friend, who had saved their lives. And do you know who that baby Walker was? It was Mr. Underwood's great-great-great grandfather."

There was a chorus of "Wow!" and "That's great!" and "Is that true, Mr. Underwood? Is it really true?"

Bret looked somewhat embarrassed to find himself the unwitting star of the story, but he replied, "If your teacher says it's true, you'd better believe it. Every word."

And he murmured in Dani's ear, "I don't think there were any bears in this part of the country back then."

She widened her eyes at him. "Are you calling your own grandmother a liar?"

He grinned. "You are amazing. Absolutely amazing."

Dani gave him a flirtatious toss of her head and replied, "And it's about time you realized it, too." She jumped lightly to the ground and brushed off the back of her coat. "All right, children, finish up your lunches. You know what to do with your trash, don't you?''

Anne was already passing among them with a plastic bag, but most of the children had been so entranced by the story, they had not even begun their lunches yet. Dani didn't rush them. She was no more anxious to get back to the schoolroom than they were. She walked out of the shelter of the trees, tilting her face up to catch the sprinkles of snow, and thought about Hannah and Zaccariah Underwood, who had come here so long ago and endured so much hardship for the sake of this land. On days like this, they were so close, she could almost touch them.

Bret stood beside her. "If they had the whole state to choose from," he commented, following her thoughts, "looks like they could have picked a better piece of land than this one."

Dani shot him a dry look. "They did, as you know perfectly well. This whole county and more was Underwood land at one time or another."

"Figures they'd end up with the only uncultivatable plot this side of the Rockies. But, then, what can you expect from a family that started out with a couple of greenhorns who didn't even have enough sense to bring provisions with them to last through the winter?"

"Honestly, Bret, you're impossible. Don't you have any pride in your heritage at all?"

"Nope," he replied cheerfully.

She caught the glint in his eye and knew that he was teasing her, but the fact mollified her only slightly.

"You're a disgrace to your name," she grumbled.

"I do my best."

Dani's eyes moved to the old oak tree, and she tried not to be too irritated with Bret about his cavalier attitude toward a past that, to her, was more magical than Christmas. As close as they were, there were some things about him she would never understand, and knowing that disturbed her.

But suddenly, she caught his hand. "Bret, look!"

He followed her upraised arm in some confusion. "What?"

"Mom, Dad," Dani called over her shoulder, "watch the kids for a minute, will you? We'll be right back." She tugged at Bret's hand.

"What?" he demanded. "Where are we going?"

"Mistletoe!" she exclaimed, and she broke into a run, pulling Bret across the snow-dusted field beside her.

Chapter Seven

The mistletoe was nestled in the fork of a thick branch midway up the oak tree. Dani stopped beneath it, panting a little as she pointed upward. "Right up there, do you see? Climb up and get it for me, will you Bret?"

He turned an incredulous gaze on her. "Oh, yeah, right. Just shimmy a hundred feet up a tree in the middle of a snow storm."

"It's not a hundred feet!" Then she said impatiently, "Oh, all right, I'll do it." She reached for a low branch of the tree. "Just give me a boost."

He stared at her for a moment, then announced, "You're crazy." He took her shoulders and moved her firmly aside, grabbing hold of the branch himself. "I'll probably break my neck." He swung himself up.

"Be careful," Dani said, and he spared her a dark look as he reached for a handhold on the next branch.

Dani stepped back, clasping her hands behind her back, tilting her head back to follow his progress. "Do you know the legend of the mistletoe?" she said conversationally.

The branches creaked and rustled with the remnants of a few dead leaves as he made his way upward. "Yeah, it has to do with somebody getting murdered, doesn't it?"

"It does not."

"Sure it does. The man who shot Achilles in the heel used a mistletoe arrow, and the stuff has been killing innocent men who climb up slippery trees ever since."

She choked back a giggle. "That's the most unromantic thing I've ever heard."

"You want romantic? I'll tell you what romantic is. Romantic is Carmel Beach at sunset. Romantic is sitting by a fire with a glass of wine. Romantic is not—"

A branch snapped suddenly and Dani's breath caught in her throat, her hand going up automatically as though to shield him from a fall. But Bret continued easily, "I repeat, romantic is *not* freezing to death in the top of a tree trying to snag mistletoe for some...silly...woman."

The last few words were punctuated with grunts of exertion as Bret strained to reach the cluster of mistletoe and detach it from the branch. Suddenly, the cluster came free and tumbled through the tree limbs, raining berries and leaves and fragile, broken stems amidst Dani's shouts of delight.

She stretched her hands upward to catch the cluster, laughing. "My hero!" she called.

Bret grinned down at her, his feet braced on a sturdy limb and his hand balanced on a branch above him. Dani thought if ever there had been a picture-perfect portrait of a hero, it would be him. His hair frosted with snow, his eyes twinkling like sunshine, his broad shoulders and well-fitting jeans...he looked like a woodland god, poised up there in the tree, master of all he surveyed. The sight of him made Dani's heart catch for a minute, like a schoolgirl struck by the glimpse of a fantasy come to life.

He began to descend the branches, and in a moment, he sprang to the ground beside her. His face was slightly flushed with exertion, and his eyes danced with sparks of light.

"Well done!" she said, applauding him. "I'm glad to see you haven't forgotten everything I taught you."

"I'd make old Walks-Among-Trees proud, wouldn't I?" he agreed. "You've got that junk all in your hair."

"*That's* the mistletoe legend I was referring to," she replied pertly. She reached up her hand to pull the stems and leaves out of her hair, but Bret moved to do the same thing at the same time, and their fingers became entangled.

He said softly, "Do you mean the one about kissing?"

Their eyes met. Their fingers twined together lightly and did not move. The moment between them was poised and expectant, and either one of them, with a word, a breath, a shifted gaze, could have broken it. But no power on earth could have persuaded Dani to move away from Bret then.

She whispered, "Absolutely."

Their lips touched, as they had done many times before, but both of them knew from the first instant that this time was different. The memory of Bret's eyes just before he lowered his face to hers swirled in Dani's head—the surprise, the quick darkening of intensity, the same spark of irresistible excitement and curiosity that quickened in Dani's own veins. Her heartbeat took on a breathless, leaping rhythm even before his lips touched hers and when they did, it was with a rush of heat and weakness she had not expected.

His kiss went through her like something liquid and shimmering, stroking nerve endings into a sudden shock of awareness, flooding her with warmth, taking away her breath. Not the kiss of a friend, not a brief affectionate embrace, but a natural melding of man and woman, a chain reaction of swift-flowing sparks, of bodies coming together in perfect chemistry and muted wonder. Dani realized dizzily that she had waited all her life for this kiss.

There was surprise, yes, for both of them, but it was more like something that caught them off guard than something that was completely unexpected, for they both must have known deep in their hearts and secret memories that it would be like this. Every sensory receptor in Dani's body seemed to suddenly energize and flare to life. She could hear the soft whisper of the snow and feel its feathery touch as it drifted down on her hair. She could smell the crisp scent of pine and the subtle, woodsy aroma of mistletoe and Bret's warm, quietly masculine fragrance—like sunshine and tanned skin. She could feel the silky texture of her own hair against her cheek and each individual tendon and bone of Bret's hand, clasped around hers. The slightly coarse texture of his chin, the cottony softness of his jacket, the cold air around them and the pocket of heat they created between them, and Bret, who invaded every part of her with his touch, his kiss.

She could feel his restraint, even as she struggled with her own. Their entwined fingers, which were resting against the curve of Dani's neck, tightened briefly and then slowly, deliberately released. And even as they separated, the kiss seemed to linger, breaths mingling and heat flowing as they gradually, a fraction of an inch at a time, moved apart.

Dani's heart was pounding so forcefully that she thought he must surely be able to hear it, or see it, shaking her rib cage. She could feel the color staining her cheeks and see it in his, and for the longest time, all she could do was stare at him. She saw in his eyes the same kind of slow, pleasured astonishment that she felt, as though he couldn't believe what had just happened or understand why, as though he didn't know what to say or feel or whether he should apologize or she should....

And she wouldn't. Her head was spinning, and her emotions were like a tangled skein of yarn that grew more tightly knotted the harder she tried to sort them out. She only knew that she could not think about it now. She could not risk this moment.

She turned away, brushing the last of the mistletoe out of her hair. "We'd better be getting back," she said brightly. "They'll send out a search party."

He didn't answer.

She glanced at him quickly and made no effort to disguise the pleading in her eyes. *Not now, Bret. Don't talk about it now....*

But aloud she said, with that same false, almost frenetic cheer, "Tree-trimming party tonight. First course at Mom's, dessert at my house. No begging off. It's a tradition."

He hesitated, and then he forced a smile. "Right. Wouldn't miss it."

He dropped a hand atop her shoulder in an exaggerated gesture of companionability, and together, they walked back to the others.

THE AFTERNOON PASSED IN A blur of schoolroom colors, of construction-paper chains and the smell of wheat paste, popcorn strings and the sound of childish excitement. Dani felt a semblance of that excitement inside, and it had nothing to do with the pine tree in the corner that was gradually transformed with paper birds and homemade ornaments into a Christmas spectacle. She felt feverish, a little breathless, distracted and delighted. She also felt disturbed and confused and very guilty.

She wasn't guilty for having kissed Bret, nor was she sorry. She wasn't even guilty for having enjoyed it. And that, in truth, was exactly what she did feel guilty about. Because in that one delirious moment when the whole world seemed to open beneath her feet, past and present flowing together to form nothing but an endless vista of possibilities, she had not thought of anyone or anything at all except Bret. And that was very wrong. And very confusing.

After school, she held a rehearsal for the play, but it wasn't easy to keep her mind on what she was doing. Finally, she asked Paula to take over and she went to call Todd. The sound of his voice should have been reassuring, but it wasn't.

"Christmas party tonight," she announced brightly. "Want to come?"

"What? Nobody told me. Or did I forget?"

"Well, it's not really a party," she admitted. "Just tree trimming and eggnog with the folks. But I'd really like you to come, Todd. We've never done that together."

There was a pause. "Ah, honey, you know I'd like to, but it's kind of short notice. I was planning to work late."

Dani tried to feel disappointment. She really did. "No problem, I understand. Just thought it was worth a try. We'll miss you."

"Not as much as I'll miss you."

She forced a smile, even though he couldn't see.

"Say, how did I do last night?"

She blinked. "What?"

"With your friend. Did I pass?"

She swallowed hard and pushed the smile back into her voice. "With flying colors."

"Ha! The master at work!"

"Listen," she said quickly, "I've got a stage full of kids waiting for me, and you need to get back to work. Call me this weekend, okay?"

"Sure thing. Bye, sweetheart."

She went back to the cafeteria, feeling no calmer than when she had left, yet with a strange pricking emptiness inside she couldn't quite explain.

She loved Todd. She knew she did. Why should anything be different just because Bret had kissed her?

No... because they had kissed each other, willingly, thoroughly and as adults. Because they had wanted to. And they had enjoyed it. More than enjoyed it...

She cut rehearsal short and promised herself she would make it up next week. Pauline gathered up her sheet music and came over to Dani as she was stuffing her papers harum-scarum back into her briefcase.

"You feeling okay?"

Dani wouldn't look at her. "Why? Don't I look okay?"

"You look like a woman with something on her mind." Pauline sat down at the small table, hands folded patiently. "So, what is it?"

Dani hesitated, then sighed. She sat down, too. "Pauline," she said carefully, "with men, even when they're married—happily married—they can still be attracted to other women, can't they?"

"Oh-oh." Pauline's eyes rounded. "Todd's got a roving eye already?"

Dani shook her head impatiently. "No, what I'm trying to say is—do you think it's possible, even if you're really in love with somebody, to be—well, attracted to someone else?"

"Of course, it is," Pauline responded immediately. "That's what God made fantasies for."

Dani tried to keep the anxiety out of her voice. "And it's okay. I mean, it's perfectly normal."

Her friend shrugged. "Sure it is. I don't care if I was married to a guy with the sex appeal of a rock star and the sensitivity of a talk-show host, if some twenty-three-year-old Adonis walks by in a French bikini, I'm going to look."

"And lust?"

She grinned. "And lust."

Dani took a breath. That was all it was, and it was completely understandable. Bret was an incredibly attractive man; what woman wouldn't, if given half a chance, succumb to his charms? Could she be blamed for her curiosity, hormones or whatever impulse had prompted her to step into his embrace? There was nothing to be ashamed of. It had all been perfectly harmless.

Pauline reached out and patted Dani's hand. "Listen, you want some advice? You're not married yet. You're not even engaged. Let Todd get it out of his system. As long as he's just *attracted* to other women, neither one of you has anything to be worried about. But if it's more than that... well, he—and you—deserve the chance to find out. You know what I mean?"

Dani nodded slowly. *If it's more than that...*

Pauline grinned and got to her feet. "This from a woman who's been divorced twice. You sure know where to go for advice, friend. Let me know if I can do anything else to help."

"Thanks, Pauline," Dani murmured absently. "I'll see you tomorrow."

Pauline laughed and waved on her way out the door. "I hope not! Tomorrow's Saturday."

Dani was thoughtful but a great deal more composed as she made her way home. She had never been given to self-deception, and she was not going to try to convince herself now that what had happened between her and Bret was an accident, an aberration, something to be forgotten and ignored. The truth was, she had wanted his kiss, she had not turned away from it, and it had been wonderful. And the further truth was that it was only natural that she would want to know whether or not anything remained of the old school crushes she had had on him. She had her answer now, and it shouldn't surprise her. Bret was very sexy; he always had been and always would be. There was nothing wrong about the surface attraction she felt for him... as long as that was all it was. And that *was* all it was.

She was almost sure of it.

BRET REMEMBERED VERY well the traditional tree-trimming buffet at the Griffin household. Cold cuts, sliced pumpernickel, homemade bread-and-butter pickles—anything that could be eaten with the fingers between trips to the ornament boxes, because Anne had learned early on that it was impossible to keep the children seated at the table for the length of a meal when there was a tree waiting in the living room and boxes full of Christmas magic to be unearthed. There were no children anymore, but the excitement was just as high as it had been twenty years ago, and the warmth of memories was contagious.

Bret stayed busy in the kitchen with his own soon-to-be-famous eggnog recipe while Dani helped her mother tack evergreen boughs and bright red bows over the doorways and along the banister, and Harold grumbled and mumbled over the strings of lights. Bret assured himself that he wasn't avoiding Dani. There was nothing to feel awkward about. He wasn't ashamed of what had happened beneath the oak tree, and he wasn't going to apologize for it.

The last thing he intended to do was apologize for it.

He carried the big bowl of eggnog into the living room and announced, "All right, friends and neighbors, prepare yourselves for the taste sensation of a lifetime. From your own living room to the shelves of finer food stores everywhere, this may be your last chance."

"After a buildup like that, how can we refuse?" declared Anne.

Harold abandoned a tangled string of lights and agreed, "Sounds like just what the doctor ordered to get me through the night."

Dani picked her way carefully around the strings of lights and boxes of ornaments spread out over the floor. "Don't believe a word of it. He used a mix."

Bret pretended insult. "If you were a man, I'd call you out for that."

Dani made a face at him.

The same old Dani...and not. Just looking at her filled him with delight, as it always did. She was wearing faded jeans that hugged her thighs and her rounded bottom in an intimate, hard-to-ignore way, and a red sweatshirt with a Santa face painted in white on the front. Her hair swung in a glossy pony tail that fell just below her ears, and her eyes twinkled with the familiar playful mischief. But were her eyes a little brighter when she looked at him now, her cheeks a little more flushed? Bret knew it probably wasn't right, but he found himself hoping so.

He ceremoniously dipped the thick creamy mixture into cups, receiving the elder Griffins' enthusiastic compliments and Dani's noncommittal, "Not bad . . . for a California boy." They filled paper plates with selections from the buffet, and Bret sat on the floor beside a cardboard box marked "Xmas," pulling out ornaments between bites of ham and cheese.

"I think we should have gotten a bigger tree," he commented.

Dani sat cross-legged on the floor before him, balancing her plate on one knee. "Some of them are for my tree," she told him. "Mom's going through this designer phase—she only uses pink and red on her tree."

"And it's always perfectly beautiful," Anne said proudly.

"Yeah, for a department-store window," Dani shot back. "I prefer a more eclectic look."

Bret chuckled. "You would."

They smiled at each other, caught in one of those moments of perfect understanding that only a lifetime of shared memories can produce, an intimacy of knowledge that encompasses good and bad, faults and weaknesses, and accepts without question. That was what they had, Bret and Dani, and it had survived far more challenging episodes than a kiss in the snow. They smiled at each other, and suddenly, everything was all right.

Bret pulled out a ceramic bell ornament, a little chipped in places, its paint fading. "Your tree," he decided.

"Right." Dani dug into the box and came up with a pink velvet bow carefully wrapped in tissue. "Mom's tree."

They began to sort the ornaments into two separate piles, and Dani said, "You look ten years younger."

He looked at her in surprise. "What?"

"Than when you first got here," she explained. "Well, maybe not ten years, but two, at least."

Her mother laughed, but agreed, "She's right, Bret. I think the country air is good for you."

He shrugged. "I don't know about that. But I do know I've had more fun today than I have in a long time." He was surprised to hear himself say that, even more surprised to realize it was true. All these hokey Christmas traditions, the kids with all their noise and unpredictability, the snow falling in the woods and the smell of fresh-cut pine... and that wondrous, joyous moment of discovery and disbelief when he had taken Dani in his arms. It was all part of the magic, not one element separable from the others. It was a package of memories, and he knew he would be able to taste the texture of this day for years to come.

He was aware of Dani looking at him thoughtfully, but she did not look as surprised by his admission as he was. And, of course, she wouldn't be. He always had said Dani knew him better than he knew himself.

Then Anne said, "What do you usually do for Christmas, Bret?"

He chuckled and shook his head. "I'm embarrassed to say."

The solemn look vanished from Dani's face as she teased, "It's something lewd. I knew it would be."

"Dani!" Anne reprimanded.

Bret grinned at her. "I go sailing," he confessed. "I know it sounds pagan, but that's what I do—when I can take the time off from work, that is. This friend of mine has a boat, and hardly anybody else is on the water on Christmas day, so..."

"All by yourself?" inquired Anne, looking distressed.

"Usually."

"All alone in a boat on Christmas day...that's the saddest thing I ever heard."

"Oh, leave the boy alone, Mother Hen," Harold told her. "A man likes to get off by himself once in a while. Many's a Christmas afternoon I've spent out in a deer stand—"

"But you always had your family, and the tree in the morning, and Christmas dinner together..." Anne broke off, shaking her head. "I'm sorry Bret, I am an interfering old mother hen. But it *is* sad, I don't care what anybody says. And if I had known that's how you spent Christmas, I would've made sure you came home a long time before now."

Dani grinned at Bret. "That's right, Oliver Twist, play it for all it's worth. Poor abandoned boy, all alone on some playboy's yacht, nothing but champagne and smoked salmon for his Christmas dinner, nothing but the false glitter of the distant lights of Catalina to guide him...."

Bret threw a handful of tinsel at her. "I'm starting to remember why I prefer spending Christmas by myself."

The tinsel caught like stardust in her hair, and Dani pulled it out, throwing it back at him strand by strand until Anne broke up the fight with some exasperated comment about children.

It was Christmas like a dozen other Christmases before it, with Harold admonishing Bret to "Check this bulb—no, the other one" and Anne scolding Dani for tossing the tinsel on by handfuls instead of draping it one strand at a time, and Dani finally giving up and going to the piano, keeping them all entertained with Christmas carols while the work went on much faster without her. Then there was the magical moment when the room lights were turned out and the Christmas tree was lit, and when they stood bathed in the blinking pink-and-silver glow of the tree, Dani's hand slipped quite naturally into Bret's and she leaned her head against his shoulder. A magical moment.

They boxed up the leftover ornaments and lights and trooped across the snow-frosted lawn to Dani's house, where they began it all again. They ate home-made ginger cookies—one of Dani's specialties—and drank cinnamon-spiced coffee and hot chocolate. Dani thoroughly enjoyed herself as she gave specific orders as to how *her* tree was to be decorated, which was as gaily haphazard as possible.

It was after eleven when the elder Griffins, pleading exhaustion, left Bret and Dani to put the finishing touches on the tree—the last few ornaments to be hung, the last few handfuls of tinsel to be tossed. Bret sat on the floor with a fire crackling in the grate behind him and the smell of pine filling the room, as he threaded a hanger into a gray felt mouse. The little ornament must have been twenty years old, its whiskers were crushed and one ear was missing, but Dani insisted absolutely nothing was to be left in the box.

"What does your mother want for Christmas?" Bret asked. "I want to get her something really nice."

"A pressure cooker." Dani took aim at a high branch and tossed a handful of tinsel as though it were a softball. "She wants a new pressure cooker. They have them on sale at the hardware store."

Bret made a face. "That's no kind of present for a woman."

"What's wrong with it?"

"I'm not getting her a pressure cooker."

"That's what she wants."

"I'm not getting her a pressure cooker."

Dani shrugged. "There's always that diamond bracelet she's had her eye on in the Tiffany catalog."

"I'm serious."

"So am I. A pressure cooker is about the best you're going to do around here. Todd's taking Mom and me to Centerville for shopping next weekend. Do you want to come?"

Bret placed the mouse on a low branch and reached for the last ornament. It was a miniature silver bell that made a tinny tinkling sound in his hand. There must have been three dozen such bells on Dani's tree.

"Why Centerville?" he inquired. "It's not much bigger than Clayville."

"Oh, that's right, you haven't been there since they redid it. It's the cutest little tourist trap now—all the storefronts are done in turn-of-the-century, and the streets are cobblestone. It's a great place to find all kinds of unusual gifts." She stepped back to observe the tree. "Todd keeps trying to talk to the town council about doing something like that here. It's really been great for Centerville's economy. The only trouble is, we don't have anything to make a tourist attraction out of."

Bret felt himself tensing every time she mentioned Todd's name, but she seemed perfectly unselfconscious about it. And that was sensible. The kiss they had shared that afternoon was an accident, a harmless exchange of affection that had drifted, for a moment, beyond the borders of friendship, and he would have felt terrible if Dani allowed herself to feel guilty about it. There was no reason at all he should feel hurt that she appeared to have forgotten it, but he did not want to talk about Todd any longer.

He stood up to place the bell on the end of a middle branch. It made a pleasant jingling sound and winked with sparks of firelight as it bounced on the branch. "You and your bells," he said. "I don't guess I ever think of Christmas that I don't think of bells."

"Okay, the lights," she said excitedly. She ran to the switch and turned off the other lights. "Plug them in."

For a moment, the room was illuminated only by the glow of the fire and the glitter of tinsel, and then Bret made the connection between outlet and plug. The tree sprang to life in a twinkling, blinking network of red, blue, yellow and orange.

Dani stood beside him. "Now *that's* a tree," she declared in satisfaction.

He chuckled. "I suppose it would be unnecessary to point out that having two trees—one for you and one for your folks—is a little silly. You can only have Christmas in one place."

"Just another symbol of my independence," she said. "Besides, I like it—I like decorating it and looking at it. And, tell the truth, my tree *is* prettier than Mom's, isn't it?"

Dani's tree was gaudy and overdone, so heavily decorated in places that the branches sagged. There was no color scheme or theme, just a gay collection of random memories and treasured tradition without order or plan, spontaneous, colorful and energetic, just as Christmas was supposed to be. Just as Dani was.

Bret grinned at her. "It's you," he admitted.

"There's some coffee left. Do you want some?" She started toward the kitchen.

"No, I've still got some cocoa left." He sank to the hearth and picked up his half-empty cup. "I wouldn't mind another one of those cookies, though."

"You're going to get fat."

"No chance, the way I've been working." He propped a cushion behind his shoulders and leaned back against the warm stones of the hearth, drowsy and content. "I never thought I'd say this, but that's what I miss about farm life. Getting outdoors, doing something with my hands and my own two legs.... Not that cutting down trees is a particularly noble calling, but that was fun today. And tonight, I'm going to go to bed tired, which is something I haven't done in a long time. Working out in the gym just isn't the same."

Dani placed the platter of cookies on the hearth and sat in front of him on the floor, drawing up her knees, sipping her coffee. "Is that why you've been unhappy?" she asked. "Is it your work?"

He hesitated and she thought he wouldn't answer. Then he glanced down at the cocoa in his cup and replied, "I guess. That and midlife crisis."

"You're too young to have midlife crisis."

He sipped the cocoa. "It's not just work. Nothing is turning out like I planned."

"You have everything you wanted," Dani reminded him. "You wanted to be successful, in charge, make lots of money...."

He looked at her thoughtfully. "Is that what I wanted?"

"That's what you told me."

"Then I guess you're right. I must be happy."

"Why did you come back here, Bret?" she asked gently.

He could have told her then. The firelight, the twinkling, dancing glow of the Christmas tree, and Dani sitting so close, looking at him so tenderly...it was the perfect time. But the taste of her lips was still too fresh, the firelight was too soothing, and she was too lovely.

He said, "I'm not sure." He put the cup on the hearth. "But I know I'd better be getting to bed now, before I fall asleep on your floor. We'd have a hell of a time explaining *that* to your parents."

He started to rise, and Dani had every intention of walking him to the door and telling him good-night. But instead, her hand came out to rest upon his knee, staying his movement, and once it was done, she wasn't sorry. It seemed that everything that had happened today, everything, perhaps, that had happened from the moment she looked up from her schoolroom to see him standing there, had been leading to this moment—this quiet warmth, this understanding, this intimacy. She could not let him go. She could not pretend that they had not been on the verge of discovering something new this afternoon. She couldn't pretend it had never happened. If she ignored it, it would haunt her the rest of her life. If she denied it, she would never know for sure what it was she was hiding from...and she simply had to know. Because wondering would cloud her future for as long as she lived.

Bret looked down at her hand, resting lightly on his thigh, and she could feel his muscles tense involuntarily. Her heart was beating hard and fast. She said softly, "Bret, did you ever wonder...what it might have been like between us?"

He looked at her and she saw surprise there, followed by uncertainty and a jumble of possible answers flickering through his mind, some flippant, some not. He swallowed. He said uncomfortably, "Come on, Dani, it's late."

His refusal to answer, instead of frustrating her, only made her heart beat faster with a secret, unexpected excitement. He made no move to rise, and she held his gaze, insisting on an answer.

And eventually, he gave her one because they could not lie to each other. He glanced away briefly, then back at her again. His voice was a little husky as he answered, "Of course, I have. I spent most of puberty wondering."

"Lately, I mean." She felt breathless. "When we were adults."

His eyes were steady, troubled, yet lit with a dozen conflicting little flames. Dani was lost in his gaze, seeing things there she had never expected to see before, uncertain and exhilarated and a little scared.

"I've thought about it," he said lowly. His words were rushed, almost clipped, but the tenor of them went through Dani with a little thrill, like wind moving through the aspens. "You're a sexy woman, Dani, I've always thought so. Of course I'm attracted to you, any man would be. And your Todd is a lucky man. And I don't think we should talk about this anymore."

He thought the mention of Todd's name would break the spell, but it didn't. He started to get up, but Dani's eyes held him, glowing and intense in the firelight, her fingers like a brand on his thigh. He couldn't move.

She said softly, unblinkingly, "Bret . . . kiss me."

His heart lurched in his chest. He said, with difficulty, "Dani, listen. This afternoon—"

"I know." Her words came out in a rush, backed with breathlessness, and he could see the color in her cheeks that was more than the glow of the fire. "I know, it shouldn't have happened, and maybe it was a mistake, and maybe it was just the snow and the romance of it all, but I've got to know for sure, don't you see? I can't spend the rest of my life wondering if I imagined it, I've got to—"

He had every intention of getting up and walking away; he even moved to do so, but suddenly, before she had even finished speaking, his mouth was on hers. And this time, there was no restraint; there couldn't have been even if he had wanted it.

Dani knew the minute he touched her that the kiss they had shared that afternoon was not an accident, a mistake or a trick of imagination...and she must have known all along that the only mistake was in coming to him again, risking the fire again. But she was as helpless as any moth that had ever danced around the flame as the brightness flared inside her, as Bret's mouth covered hers.

There was no gentleness this time, no hesitance or uncertainty. Bret slid down on the floor beside her, and his hands were hard on her back as he pulled her close. Her lips parted with a helpless breath and she tasted his tongue; she felt the hot, dark flush of passion and the secret invasion, the power and the wonder of physical intimacy. She was trembling inside, hot and dizzy and breathless with the suddenness of sensory shock. And only then did she realize how many times she had dreamed it might be like this with Bret.

Her hands moved along his arms and to his shoulders, then dropped weakly to rest against his chest. She could feel the strain of his muscles and the beating of his heart. She could feel the heat and the dampness of his skin against hers, the tingling and hardening of her nipples in response to him. And no, it did not feel like a betrayal. It felt as right and as natural as anything she had ever done in her life. And it was for that reason that it was so frightening.

Bret broke away almost roughly. His hands tightened for a moment on her arms and then released them abruptly. Dani could hear his unsteady breathing through the roaring in her head, and she felt weak and ill with the sudden absence of him. It was a moment before she could make herself open her eyes and look at him.

His face was flushed and sheened with perspiration, his eyes dark and quick with passion he could not hide. Dani knew that look. She had just never expected to see it on Bret's face. And she knew the look was reflected on her own. The thrill of need, the shock of wonder, the question...

The question that had only one answer.

Bret looked away from her. He said in an almost steady voice, "I trust the experiment was a success."

Dani caught her breath on a sudden stab of hurt and brought her fingers to her mouth. Her lips felt swollen, still damp with his moisture. She could still taste him inside her, still feel the gentle abrasion of his skin on her cheek. All she wanted to do was to lean her head against his chest, to feel the comfort of his arms around her. She was in tumult inside; she needed him. But he was the last person to whom she could turn now.

She whispered, "It—it wasn't an experiment."

He turned on her harshly. "What was it, then? A comparison test?"

She saw the flash of remorse on his face even as the words were spoken, even as she pressed her lips together against the shock, the pain. And then, he stood abruptly.

"I'd better go," he mumbled, not looking at her.

Dani's limbs were still trembling as she stood up, her chest still aching. But her heart was pounding now with alarm, with emptiness, with fear. "Bret—don't be mad."

"I'm not mad."

He went to the coatrack and fumbled for his coat. Dani followed him quickly, touching his arm. His muscles jerked as though she had burned him, and his jaw tightened. And then his shoulders forcibly relaxed. He retrieved his coat, but he wouldn't look at her.

"I'm not mad," he repeated more evenly. "I'm embarrassed, okay? And sorry, because I don't want you to think—"

"I won't," she insisted quickly, ready to promise him anything, ready to plead for anything, as long as he didn't despise her for this, as long as he didn't leave her with the residue of his anger filling up the ache in her chest.

He looked at her then. There was strain in the tight lines of his face and sorrow in his eyes and confusion and an awful kind of defeat. "Look," he said with difficulty. "It was a mistake coming back here. I've got things going on in my life that you don't understand—that even I don't understand. It's not fair to make you the victim of them. I think . . . I think it's probably best if I just went home. Back to Los Angeles."

The slamming of her heart was like an explosion in her chest. For a moment, she couldn't get her breath. "No!" she gasped.

And then she had to turn away because she didn't want him to see the desperation in her eyes or the struggle it took to compose herself. She pushed her fingers through the hair at her temples, drawing a deep breath, trying to marshal her wildly crashing thoughts and emotions. Finally, she managed to say tightly, "Don't do this to me—to us. Don't make me think I've driven you away and make us remember this like a—like a wall that will be between us for the rest of our lives."

She took another breath and made herself turn to face him. Her cheeks were scorched. She felt miserable and hurting inside. "Bret, I'm the one who's sorry. It was my fault, and it was stupid, and...don't let it come between us. Stay and enjoy Christmas and— Can't we forget it ever happened?"

Even as she spoke, she knew the impossibility of the suggestion, and his sober gaze reflected it. "No," he replied. "I don't think so."

Because neither of them wanted to. Because forgetting was the last thing Dani wanted to do, even though it made no sense, even though there was no point to remembering, even though it complicated her life unbearably.... She couldn't forget.

Her fists closed at her sides to still the trembling and she said, "Then—we can deal with it. We're both adults. These things happen."

The fleeting corner of a smile caught his lips, then vanished. And his eyes darkened again with the weight of anxiety. "Dani," he said quietly, "you've got your life together now. I'd never forgive myself if I thought I did anything to mess it up."

She shook her head adamantly. "You won't. You didn't. I promise."

The anxiety didn't fade. "I don't want anything to change between us, Dani."

She took an unsteady breath. "It won't, unless we let it."

She watched him, her breath stilled in her throat and expectation straining every muscle, hoping the words would be enough. Then at last, he nodded and slipped on his jacket. He even managed a smile, though it didn't quite reach his eyes. "I don't really want to go back to Los Angeles," he said. "Not before your mom's Christmas turkey, anyway."

Dani returned his smile, weak with relief. "Good night, Bret."

Any other time, he would have kissed her goodnight or she would have reached for him. But this time, he merely opened the door, said, "Lock up behind me," and then didn't look at her again as he left.

Dani closed the door and leaned against it, staring blankly at the shifting, dancing glow of the Christmas-tree lights. Their last words seemed to echo hollowly around the room, empty reassurances, frail comforts. She couldn't forget, not if she lived to be a hundred would she forget the way it felt to be in Bret's arms; she would dream about it, she would muse about it, she would grow hot thinking about it at unexpected moments of the day, and she would yearn over it for a long, long time. Everything was changed. She knew that.

And she suspected Bret knew it, too.

Chapter Eight

Bret walked over to the Skinner place—his old house—by himself the next morning. He followed the path through the woods they had taken the day before with the children, even though there was a shorter route across the fields that he and Dani used to take on their bicycles. But to go that way meant going past her house, and he didn't want to take the chance of running into her.

He couldn't believe that he was up before she was for once, and in fact, thought that was unlikely. She had probably been awake for hours, just as he had been, waiting for daylight and wondering how she was going to avoid seeing him today.

He still got flashes of hot and cold when he thought about the night before, of how close he had come to making love to her there, on the floor beneath the Christmas tree. Of how much he had wanted to. Hundreds of available women, thousands in the world, and he had to pick Dani on whom to vent his sexual urges. Dani, the most important woman in the world to him. Dani, who was in love with another man. Dani, for whom he could do nothing but ruin her life.

He still didn't understand how it had happened, how he had let it happen. Of course, Dani was uncertain and confused; who wouldn't be at a time like this? He had felt the same way right before he got married, which was why he had imagined so much more into that kiss Dani had given him all those years ago than there had been. He *had* imagined it, hadn't he? Or was it possible that even then...

But he refused to think about it any more, to let things get any further out of hand than they were already. He wasn't twenty years old anymore. Dani and he had too much history between them, precious history, to risk destroying everything for one moment of self-indulgent passion. His first instinct had been right; he should just go home and get out of her way, let her get on with her life.

But he couldn't do that. Dani was right, if he ran away now, it would only enhance the whole episode, it would make her feel guilty and make him feel worse, and they would never get past it. Their relationship had survived over twenty turbulent years of change and growth; they had too much at stake to let one indiscretion destroy it now. Somehow, they would work through this.

But he could still taste her warmth, and even the memory of her softness beneath his hands brought a tingle of excitement to his skin. He just didn't know how he was going to face her again.

The morning was cold and damp, fogged with ice crystals and miserably gray. Patches of snow had frozen in places and crunched beneath his feet, chilling him even through Harold's heavy boots. Faraway, a distant machine hummed—a chain saw or a tractor—but otherwise, the woods were still and bleak. The walk would have been a great deal cheerier if Dani had been along; she had a way of finding beauty in even the ugliest landscape.

The tangled woods gave way to scrubby pine growth and then stubbly field as Bret emerged behind the house that had once been his home. It had been years since he had seen the place, and he didn't know what he had expected, but the flood of memories caught him off guard.

It was a simple frame house, two stories, not much different from the Griffins' or from any other place along the highway. It was set well back from the road and had once, very early in Bret's memory, been surrounded by a cornfield. Now it was surrounded by nothing but barren, frozen stubble and weeds. There was a screen porch on the back where Bret used to play on rainy days and where his mother used to serve lemonade in the summer. A trailing rose climbed the side of the house, and when Bret was eight, inspired by some boys' adventure story he had read, he tried to climb from his bedroom window down the trellis to the ground. He had torn gashes in his hands, legs and clothes on the thorns, and still ended up falling halfway down and breaking a rib.

The screen on the porch was rusted and torn now, and the rose was nothing but a dried, unsightly skeleton clinging to the side of the house. As he came around the side, he noticed a light was on in the kitchen, and he remembered the smell of ham frying on cold mornings and buckwheat pancakes sizzling on the griddle. The kitchen had always been a warm, yellow place, sparkling bright, smelling good. Despite himself, he felt a wave of homesickness, even though he had not thought of this house as home in years. He supposed you never got over certain feelings for the house you grew up in...nor could you ever quite resign yourself to seeing it change.

The closer he moved, the more dramatic those changes became. In his youth, the house had been painted bright yellow with green shutters. At some time over the years, the color had been changed to a battleship gray, but even that was beginning to peel and flake badly. He noticed an effort had been made to repair a sagging gutter, but one of the front shutters had been removed or had fallen off and was leaning against the side of the house. Several of the storm windows were cracked and had been covered with plastic. The roof had been patched with mismatched tiles. The paving stones that led from the garage were cracked and overgrown with dead weeds, and the garage itself was badly in need of a new coat of paint. When he started up the front steps, a chunk of badly set concrete fell out from the underpinning. How had the place gotten so run-down? He had always had an understanding with Skinner, giving him a break in the rent in exchange for maintenance on the house, and the last time he had asked about it, Harold had told him Skinner was doing a fine job. Why hadn't Harold told him about this? Bret tried not to be angry, but this was his *home*.

He pushed the bell, but it obviously didn't work. He knocked loudly. He heard movement inside and after a moment, the door opened cautiously.

The man on the other side of the door was wearing a rumpled sweatshirt and a three-day growth of beard. His hair was greasy and his eyes suspicious.

Bret said, "Mr. Skinner? I'm Bret Underwood. I hope I'm not bothering you too early."

Bret extended his hand and after a moment, the other man opened the door long enough to take it in a brief, disinterested clasp. "Yeah, my wife said you might drop by. Come to throw us out, I reckon."

"No," Bret said quickly. "I just wanted to talk to you for a minute."

"You might as well," Skinner said, meeting his eyes defiantly. "I don't have this month's rent and don't intend on getting it."

"I didn't come all the way from California to collect rent," Bret said patiently. "I just wanted to talk to you about my plans for the property."

"Ain't no business of mine." But after a moment, Skinner's shoulders slumped in resignation and he pushed the door open wider. "Guess I can't keep you out. It's your house."

Bret stepped inside, and the annoyance he felt at the state of disrepair became mitigated with dismay. His mother's "front room" as she liked to call it, which had once been so cheerily filled with overstuffed couches and polished wood tables, scatter rugs faded by the sun and crisp cotton draperies, was now all but bare. There was a spindly-legged couch with a hole in one arm and a couple of molded plastic chairs of the kind Bret always associated with dentists' offices. The coffee table, a cheap mail-order piece, was scarred and watermarked. A twisted coat hanger served as an antenna for the small black-and-white television, and Jimmy Skinner was stretched out on the bare floor in front of it, watching Saturday-morning cartoons.

"Wife's at work," Skinner said ungraciously. "Ain't no coffee. Jimmy, shut that racket off. Get outside and play."

Jimmy looked at Bret with a semblance of his father's suspicious defensiveness, and Bret smiled at him. "Hi, bud. How're you doing?"

Jimmy mumbled something in reply, then turned the television off and left the room.

"Blasted kid," Skinner muttered, "always underfoot." He sank to the sofa. "That's the trouble with kids today, they don't have enough to do. 'Course, that's the trouble with a lot of us."

Bret sat down uncertainly on one of the plastic chairs. Skinner had not offered to take his coat, and Bret was glad because it wasn't warm in the room. He could feel a draft from the front windows, where plastic substituted for a pane, and the flame on the gas heater was turned down to a feeble glow, probably to conserve money. But despite its poverty, the room was scrupulously clean, which only made it sadder somehow. That was the evidence of someone whose pride was all that was left.

Abruptly, Bret was convinced, beyond any doubt there might have been, that selling this place was the best thing he could do. He shouldn't have held on to it this long. There was nothing of his childhood left except the ghosts of memories, and the two hundred acres certainly weren't doing the Skinners any good. It would be best for everyone, just as he had always thought.

George Skinner said, "Look, I know what you come for, so no point in us sitting here staring at each other. We'll be out by the first of the year. The wife, she's about had it with me. Can't say's I blame her." He lifted the bottle again, his eyes bleak and bloodshot. "Said she'll stay till after Christmas, for the boy's sake, but after that . . ." He shrugged. "Reckon she'll be moving back with her folks, out in Minnesota. And me, I don't need a house if I don't have a family."

Then he looked at Bret, his expression abruptly anxious and his tone somewhere between a plea and a demand. "Just till after Christmas. That's all I ask. Let us stay that long."

Bret did not want to hear this. He did not want to be here. He could not recall ever having been so miserable, uncomfortable or completely at a loss in all his life. But he managed to meet the other man's eyes directly, and he said, "I'm sorry for your trouble. I know the land didn't turn out to pay like you hoped—"

Skinner waved a dismissing hand. "Weren't your fault. You never charged us a penny's rent for the land we worked, and I appreciate it, I really do. Trouble is, good land costs money, and I don't know nothing but farming." He took another drink. "Anyways, it don't concern you. You've been more than fair."

"There's no hurry about leaving," Bret said. "I just wanted to let you know I'd be putting the place on the market. When it sells, I'll give you plenty of notice before you have to vacate. Maybe..." He hesitated. "Maybe it will be good for you to move on. Find some place you can make a decent living."

The minute he spoke, Bret knew how false the words sounded and he was ashamed of them. But Skinner just mumbled, "Yeah. Maybe."

Bret got up, and Skinner walked him to the door. On the porch, Bret looked around, struck again by how sad and neglected the old house looked in the dull morning light. He said quietly, "I would've paid for the repairs."

The other man avoided his eyes. "I couldn't afford the raise in rent. We had a deal. I do the repairs, you keep the rent low. I did the best I could."

Bret felt small and miserable. He said, "I wouldn't have raised the rent."

He drew up his collar against the cold and started back home, thinking about the false glitter and tacky glamour of Los Angeles. He had never thought he would miss it, but it seemed to him a very welcoming place to be right then. Nothing very real, nothing very demanding, nothing, really, very important at all. It wasn't such a bad way to live.

On impulse, he decided to take the shortcut across the fields. But the old path had gone the way of the children who once had ridden it, and twenty feet into the field, he found himself hip deep in a tangle of briars and scrub brush. For a moment, he just stood there, letting the cold seep into his skin and bleakness chill his soul. "What a mess," he said. And he turned and fought his way back out.

BRET FOUND HAROLD WARMING up his pickup, preparing to go into work. He took one look at Bret's glum expression and said, "Yeah, I figured that's where you'd gone. I'm sorry about the shape the place is in, son. I would've talked to you about it sooner, but when you said you were going to sell..." He shrugged.

For a moment, it seemed as though there was no more to say. Then Bret spoke abruptly, "Do me a favor, will you? Check the place out and see what it needs. I didn't get a chance to look around inside much. Whatever it takes, just make out a bill. And listen, don't do the work yourself, okay? Hire Skinner to help you, whatever the going rate is. Tell him...tell him you're subcontracting and the real-estate company is paying for the work."

Harold grinned. "That's the spirit. I'll take care of it today." He started toward the truck, then looked back. "Of course, you realize we won't be able to paint until spring—"

"Aluminum siding, then."

Harold frowned. "That's an awful lot of expense for a place you're not planning to keep."

Bret knew that. The whole idea was foolish and impulsive and not the move of a good businessman at all. But he rationalized his request, saying, "If I want to sell the place, it's got to look good. So just fix it up. Whatever it takes."

The grin returned. "That'll be good news to an awful lot of men who need the work at Christmas. Not to mention what it'll do for my store. You get a discount, of course."

Bret knew that arguing with Harold would do no good, so he returned the grin, feeling a little better. "Of course."

Harold climbed inside the truck, shifting into reverse before he closed the door. "Wouldn't be surprised if we had it done in a week," he called. "You won't recognize the place!"

Bret stepped out of the way, his hands stuffed into his pockets against the cold, and replied, "That's not the point. I *want* to recognize the place."

Harold nodded his understanding, smiling, and waved as he backed out of the drive.

Bret found Anne in the kitchen, cleaning up the breakfast dishes. Never had a kitchen looked so good to him. Never had home felt so warm.

"You didn't have any breakfast," she announced as he hung his coat on the rack by the door. "Sit down, I'll fix you something."

"No, thanks, I'm not hungry." And because he knew he wouldn't get away with that, he added, "My stomach's a little upset." He forced a smile. "Too many cookies last night."

That Anne understood. "Well, have some juice, anyway. You can't go around all morning without anything at all."

Obediently, Bret took a bottle of apple juice from the refrigerator.

"By the way, your office called."

Bret stifled a groan. "I should've checked in before now. I knew something would go wrong."

"Nobody said anything was wrong. The young lady sounded very sweet and cheerful, and she said it wasn't urgent."

Bret poured the juice and returned the bottle to the refrigerator. "I'd better call her back."

"And, Bret, if you don't mind, could you take some things down to the church for me this afternoon? Just some candelabra and some poinsettias. I would've asked Harold, but they'd blow away in the back of that truck, and he won't take the car to work."

Bret smiled at her, happy to feel useful after the futility that had settled over him with the events of the morning. "Glad to. Just let me make that call."

"No hurry."

He took the glass of juice to the living room and settled back in a wing chair, using his credit card to make the call.

Linda Cranston answered on the first ring.

"What's wrong?" he demanded.

"What? No 'hi, babe?' And I thought a vacation would improve your manners."

Bret replied, "Hi, babe. What's wrong?"

"That's better. And nothing's wrong, for your information. As a matter of fact, the place never ran smoother. It's amazing what the mice can do when the cat's away—"

"Miss Cranston." His voice took on a warning note.

"Yes, Mr. Scrooge. Right away, sir."

That made him smile. It *was* good to hear her voice, to be connected for a moment to the bright, busy world in which he belonged, where everything was routine, nothing was complex and he always knew the answers. He couldn't remember, for a moment, why he had ever left.

"All I wanted to tell you," Linda went on, "was that you had a call from Craig Notions yesterday. Something about your property, I imagine. He wants you to get in touch with him."

Bret lifted an eyebrow. "Well, that's timing for you," he murmured.

"What?"

"Nothing. Listen, about the Christmas bonuses—"

"You made out the checks the first of November, remember? It's all taken care of."

He did remember, now that she mentioned it. "Right. But the schedule for Christmas day—"

—"That's taken care of, too. I know this might come as a shock to you, but the world actually does go on spinning without you turning the crank. Everything is just fine. Are you having a good time?"

Bret hesitated, not certain whether to be reassured or depressed by how little he seemed to be needed. "Yeah, sure," he answered, but he wasn't even certain whether that was true anymore. "But, listen, I was thinking—"

"If the rest of that sentence has anything to do with your coming back early," she said sternly, interrupting him, "don't say it. If you show your face here before New Year's Day, I'll quit, I swear I will. You need this vacation—almost as much as the rest of us need a vacation from you."

Bret smiled through a half-smothered sigh. "Why does it seem to be my fate to be surrounded by bossy, overbearing women?" he grumbled.

"Because you love it," she returned pertly. "Merry Christmas. And don't call me—I'll call you."

Bret's smile turned reflective as he hung up the phone. Yes, there were things he missed about California, but now, he was beginning to realize that work wasn't one of them. And Linda had unwittingly put her finger on the exact source of the dissatisfaction that had been troubling him for months: he wasn't needed there. The challenge was gone, the routine flowed uninterrupted with or without him. As George Skinner had said, everybody needs something to do.

He dialed Craig Notions's real-estate office a little absently, wondering what it was, then, that he wanted to do... and if he had ever really known.

"Do I have news for you!" Craig said boisterously when he got on the line. "You are dealing with the shrewdest, fastest broker this side of the Mississippi, and if you had a shred of decency, you'd double my commission."

"Not until I hear what you've done."

"I, my dear fellow, have all but closed the deal on your Clayville property, sight unseen. Is that a stroke of genius or what?"

Bret was stunned. "It's a stroke of something. What are you talking about?"

"The Japanese, Bret, the Japanese!" He was practically chortling. "How would you like to be the beneficiary of the excess cash flow of one of the largest electronics manufacturers in the world? We're talking millions here. Millions!"

"This is starting to sound like a scam," Bret said cautiously.

"Well," Craig conceded, "I don't expect to get millions for the property, or even close. But we will get a hell of a lot more than it's worth, and that's the name of the game, isn't it?"

"Will you cut the bull and get to the point?" That, Bret realized impatiently, was the one thing he had gotten used to in Clayville that was utterly lacking in L.A.—straight talk.

"All right, here's the deal. Inushu Electronics is looking to open a new plant in the Midwest. All they need is a highway, a couple of hundred acres and a fairly central location from which to draw their labor force. And guess what I just happened to have for sale? We've done the demographics. We've shown them the maps and the plat. They're interested. They're more than interested. They're sending a rep down next week to draw up a report."

Bret felt a little overwhelmed. And the only thing he could think of for the moment was that, if the Japanese were going to build a plant on the property, there was hardly any need to fix up the house. The first thing they'd do would be to bulldoze it.

Still, he was cautious. "Then it's hardly a done deal, is it? I mean, they've got to be looking at other pieces of real estate."

Craig sounded exasperated. "But this is the one they're going to buy. Jeez, don't overdo the gratitude, will you? You're embarrassing me."

"Sorry, Craig. It sounds great, it really does. It's just that..." But he wasn't sure what it was.

"Yeah, I know, you always were a conservative son-of-a-gun. So let's just say this is an early Christmas present. I'll get back with you as soon as we're ready to come out and look at the property. I'll tell you this, though. Be as skeptical as you want, but these guys are no fools. If they want to beat the new tax laws, they're going to have to move before the end of the year, so don't be surprised if you have a big, fat check in your stocking Christmas morning."

For a long moment after he had disconnected, Bret sat there, trying to let it sink in. Of course, nothing was certain, but this was a good thing. If it worked out, it could be a very good thing for everyone concerned, and after the rotten morning he'd had, wasn't it about time something started looking up? This was what he wanted. Why in the world should he feel even the least bit uneasy about it?

There was no reason, he decided firmly. No reason in the world. It was the best thing that could possibly happen; he couldn't have asked for more. And, as though to prove it to himself, he jumped up and started toward the kitchen. "Hey, Miss Annie!" he called. "Guess what?"

THE CHURCH WAS REDOLENT with the smell of evergreen and beeswax, rich with the glow of polished pews and the muted light that poured through the stained glass windows. It was a soothing place to be, comforting and calming—or it should have been. It would have been on any other day of Dani's life, but today, she was so bogged down in guilt and uncertainty that church was the last place she wanted to be.

She was the first of the decorating committee to arrive—except for Todd, who had come early to go over the score for the cantata they would be rehearsing that afternoon. She hadn't really planned on meeting Todd, and what he thought was a happy coincidence was, in fact, an unpleasant shock for Dani. She had wanted to be here alone, to compose herself before the others arrived, and she had wanted to get away from the house early, before she ran into Bret.... Spending the morning with Todd had not been in her plans.

But it was probably the best thing that could have happened. She was tense and distracted, and, of course, he noticed, but he never made an issue of it, never forced her hand, never let her mood affect his. He made her feel ashamed of herself in more ways than one, but more importantly, he made her remember just what a special man he was and how lucky she was to have found him at this stage of her life. When at last she mumbled some apology about too little sleep and P.M.S., he just grinned and held the ladder for her as she climbed up to tack a wreath over the door.

He was working at the piano now, the bright glow of the music lamp casting an aura around his profile, and she thought, *A saint, that's what he is. He's a saint, and I'm a fool for ever doubting for a minute that he's the man I want to marry....*

And that's what it was with Bret, she was sure. She was starting to feel overwhelmed by the choices that faced her, and she wanted to check out all her options. It wasn't as though she was the first woman in the world to feel such doubts. She had nothing to be ashamed of. She hadn't really made a commitment to Todd yet; she hadn't really betrayed him. They were both adults, and did she think for one minute that Todd hadn't slept with other women before he met her? Not, of course, that she had done anything of the sort with Bret... but that was the trouble. She had wanted to. And no amount of rationalizing or reexamining could convince her otherwise. She had wanted to make love with Bret last night, very badly, and it was he who had pulled away, not she.

She had no intention of telling Todd about it, but she had an awful feeling that if she did, he would understand. It was Bret she was worried about. She had thrown herself at him. She had behaved like a wanton, sex-starved teenager. What must he think of her now? She was supposed to be in love with another man, yet she had gone into Bret's arms without a moment's thought or hesitation or even a twinge of guilt.

She felt plenty of guilt now. She felt guilty for Todd's sake, because if he had been with another woman after all they had shared, she would never have forgiven him. She had no right to expect better from him on her behalf—but she did. She felt guilty for her own sake because it wasn't like her to behave like that, and she didn't understand what had come over her. But most important, she felt guilty for Bret's sake. She had almost driven him away. What was he thinking now? How could she ever face him again?

She had an opportunity to find out sooner than she expected or even wanted. She was tacking garlands of fresh evergreen along the choir loft when she heard the vestibule door open. She turned, expecting to see the rest of the decorating committee. Instead, Bret stood there, holding a potted poinsettia beneath each arm and balancing a candelabrum in either hand.

He looked as surprised to see her as Dani was to see him, and for a moment, she was helpless beneath the flood of inevitable memories. Her cheeks went hot, and her skin prickled, just as though she could feel his hands caressing it now. Her eyes were drawn to his mouth, and her stomach tightened as she remembered the swift, hot invasion of his tongue, the taste of him, the feel of him.... And he was remembering, too. She could see it in his eyes.

They both felt Todd's gaze and they broke eye contact quickly, speaking at once. Bret said, "Hi, Dani."

Dani said, "What are you doing here?"

Their voices sounded forced, a little too casual, a little too loud.

Todd got up from the piano. Dani might have noticed something strange in the glance he gave her, but his attitude was easy and relaxed as he approached Bret. "Here, let me give you a hand."

"Thanks." Bret handed over a potted plant and a candelabrum. "There're more in the car. Dani's mom sent me over with them."

"The Garden Club supplies the poinsettias for the church every year," Dani explained, wiping her hands on her skirt and hoping the gesture didn't seem too nervous. "They always end up dumping them at Mom's house."

Todd placed the poinsettia on the altar table, and Bret followed him, looking around curiously. "So, what's going on?"

"The Christmas cantata is tomorrow night." Todd took the other candelabrum from him and set it on the altar. "We're trying to get the church decorated before final rehearsal this afternoon. The other ladies should be here any minute."

"Cantata, huh?" Bret's smile seemed almost natural. "And I guess Dani's directing it."

"Actually," Dani said, coming down the steps to them, "Todd's the choir director."

Bret looked at the other man in surprise. "No kidding?"

"Just amateur," Todd admitted. "It's a volunteer job. But this year's cantata looks pretty good, if I do say so myself. You'll be here, won't you?"

"Wouldn't miss it." Bret glanced at Dani, then away before she could meet his eyes. "Well, you two do have a lot in common. Music, I mean. Dani's always been the biggest star this town ever produced. Singing, dancing, you name it."

Todd caressed the back of Dani's neck in brief affection. "She's still a star," he said.

Dani said hurriedly, "Do you want us to help you bring in the rest of the plants?"

"No, you go ahead with what you're doing. I'll get them."

But Todd followed him out, and they brought in the remainder of the poinsettias in one trip. Dani began to arrange the plants in clusters around the altar and the pulpit, and she tried to convince herself the silence wasn't too awkward. But it must have been because Bret broke it with a sudden, almost too boisterous, "Well, I had some interesting news today."

"What's that?" Dani spoke without turning.

"I think I've got an offer on my property."

Todd exclaimed, "Is that right? Well, I never would have thought you'd sell it this quickly. Who is it, someone from out of town?"

Bret chuckled. "Way out of town. The Japanese, actually. They're considering it as a possible site for a new electronics plant. Inushu—maybe you've heard of them."

Dani turned around slowly, staring at him. "You're kidding."

He shook his head. "I don't think so. It's not settled yet, of course, but my broker sounds pretty excited. They're sending someone down next week to do an on-site survey."

Dani said incredulously, "You're going to sell your property to the *Japanese?*"

"If the price is right, which I'm sure it will be."

"You'd actually *do* that?"

Bret frowned a little in confusion. "Why not? They're not communists or drug dealers or even racketeers—what's the big deal? Why are you looking at me that way?"

For a moment, Dani could only stare at him, then she stalked past him, grabbed her coat and went outside.

In only a few seconds, Bret was beside her. "What's the matter with you?" he demanded. "What did you run out here for?"

She turned on him. "Because it's a sin to fight in church! Bret, are you crazy? You're really going to sell your daddy's house to some foreign concern who's going to build an industrial *plant?*"

He still looked confused, but there was annoyance in his eyes, too. "Why not? It's not like they're going to manufacture insecticides or poisonous chemicals, but even if they were, it wouldn't have anything to do with me. Besides—"

"I don't believe you!" she cried, gesturing wildly. "I don't believe you can actually stand here and tell me you don't care about toxic waste—"

"There *isn't* any toxic waste!"

"How do you know that? How can you say that? How can you do that to your own land, the place we grew up, where your family has lived for generations! Where Zac and Hannah—"

"Spare me Zac and Hannah!" His voice rose in tone to match hers, and shoppers on the sidewalk across the street turned to stare. "For God's sake, Dani, I told you when I came here this is what I intended to do—"

"I didn't think you'd do it! You grew up here, Bret, you know—"

The door to the church opened and Todd came out. "Private conversation?" he inquired mildly.

"Tell him, Todd!" Dani demanded. "Tell him he can't do this!"

And Bret turned on him, as well. "Can you believe this woman? She's acting like I'm a war criminal or something! Do you know how many jobs a thing like this could bring to the county? New roads, new housing, not to mention outside revenue—the whole economic standard would go up two hundred percent. How can anybody possibly object to that?"

Todd said cautiously, "A thing like this could be really big news, and it certainly bears some looking into. But I've got to tell you, I'm pretty much like Dani—a traditionalist at heart. That's why I moved here. I'd hate to see things change."

Dani looked smug. "That's why *everyone* lives here," she told Bret. "Because we like the small town and the quiet life-style. If we wanted superhighways and high-rises, we'd move to the city. I can't believe you want to put an industrial plant in my backyard!"

"It's not your backyard," he told her, "it's mine. Besides, the deal isn't settled yet. It's not even a firm possibility. I thought you'd be happy for me, that's all."

"Well, I'm not!"

Bret might have responded, or Dani might have said more, but just then, a group of ladies from the decorating committee rounded the corner, calling and waving to her. Bret glanced at them and then at Dani, his jaw tight and his eyes angry. Then he said shortly, "I'll see you later." He spun on his heel and walked away.

Dani started to call him back, but let the words die unspoken. She didn't want to apologize. She wasn't sorry. She wasn't wrong. She was hurt and betrayed and angry, and why shouldn't she be?

And she was also scared. Because this wasn't the Bret she knew. Because she was afraid of losing him. And because the fight really hadn't been about the Japanese. She was shocked and angry, but that was not why she had yelled at him. She had fought with him because fighting was easier than facing up to what she had really felt when he walked into the church a few moments ago.

She greeted the members of the decorating committee automatically, and Todd draped his arm around her shoulders as they walked back inside the church. But she couldn't get over the disturbance her harsh words with Bret had left. The Christmas spirit was fading fast.

THAT AFTERNOON, ANNE WENT to rehearsal with Dani, and supper was a pot-luck affair concocted between the two men. Afterward, Harold turned on a movie on cable and invited Bret to join him, but Bret pleaded fatigue and went to his room early.

He lay on his bed with his arms folded behind his head, staring at the ceiling, angry and unhappy and trying to figure out what he had done wrong. Except that it really wasn't such a puzzle. It was all very easy to understand. Dani just couldn't accept change. She expected everything to stay the same year after year, decade after decade, handing down memories like those worn-out Christmas ornaments. But Bret was a man who thrived on change, who made changes happen, and this wasn't his home anymore.

If she couldn't accept the changes that went on in the world around her, how could she possibly be expected to accept a change in their relationship? How, for that matter, could Bret?

There was a timid knock on his door, and he turned his head toward it just as Dani pushed it open. She was carrying a small basket wrapped in red cellophane. "Peace offering," she said, indicating the basket. "Can I come in?"

He propped the pillows a little higher under his head, but didn't get up. "Only if you're carrying cookies."

"How did you guess?"

She came inside, leaving the door open a little. He could hear the drone of the television set from downstairs. She set the basket on the night table, and Bret moved his legs over, making room for her to sit beside him on the bed. It was a natural thing to do, just like old times, but when she sat beside him, he could feel his pulses speed and the scent of her perfume drifted over him like a warm caress.

"Look," she said, glancing down at her folded hands, "I feel really dumb. Mom told me how you're fixing up your house."

He said nothing.

She looked at him cautiously. "You could have called it all off after you found out about the Japanese, but you didn't. Seems like a waste. The Japanese won't have any use for the house."

He lifted one shoulder uncomfortably. "The deal might not go through. I'll need to have the place spruced up if I put it on the open market."

"Or maybe," she suggested, "you wanted to give some men around here some work and Mr. Skinner some extra money and his family a decent place to live."

She was wearing a long, bulky-knit sweater and a print skirt, hardly a sexy outfit by anybody's standards. Her hair was pulled back at her nape with a bright red bow, and she wore no makeup. She was just Dani, familiar, honest, comfortable... and beautiful.

"So I waste a little money," he said. "If I make the deal, I won't even miss it. If I don't... it can't hurt to spread a little Christmas cheer around. I'm getting tired of being called Scrooge."

"I never said you were a Scrooge."

"So now that you think I'm a sentimental tower of Jell-O, you like me again, is that it?"

She grinned. "Right."

He tilted his head to the side, examining her gravely. "Then we'd better get one thing straight. About that fight this afternoon—I was right and you were wrong."

She rolled her eyes in exasperation. "Are you going to start it all over again?"

"I just don't want any misunderstandings."

She sighed a little, looking at him with a mixture of sadness and apology. "Bret, I know that what you do with your land is your business. And I know that you really don't see anything wrong with your plans. It's just—it shocked me, that's all, to find out you felt so differently about things than I do. You're my best friend, and I guess I always assumed we thought alike on everything, and Bret, the world is changing so fast and things are so messed up that sometimes, it seems like our memories are the only things we can really count on. I just always thought that you treasured those memories as much as I do. And that's why I yelled at you."

Bret reached down and took her fingers lightly in his. "We've always thought about things a lot differently than either one of us wanted to admit." He kept his eyes on their hands, fascinated by the differences in size and texture and color. Her small, slim fingers, flower-petal white, entwined with his large brown ones, her neat, pale pink nails trimmed into delicate ovals...softness and hardness, male and female.

He raised his eyes to her face. "But you were right about one thing. You didn't mean to be, but you made me see something today, something very important. I do treasure those memories, Dani, but that's all they are—just memories, and I can't live on them. That's what makes us different—what makes me different from everybody around here, I guess. And that's why I don't belong here."

Her eyes were quick with protest. "Bret, that's not—"

But he shook his head, silencing her. "It's not that I don't want to," he went on, trying to make her understand. "There's so much about this place I love, and these last few days have been more...well, more *real* to me than anything I've done in the past five years. But I've changed too much, Dani, and I just don't fit in anymore."

"You could change back," she said gently, "if you wanted to."

He shook his head against the pillow. "I tried to change to fit into Los Angeles and I couldn't. Not really. I did a pretty good imitation, I guess, but..." He turned her hand over in his, playing with it absently, stroking the palm, curling the fingers. "You asked me yesterday about work, and I think I've figured it out. When I left here, it was to do something great, to make my mark, to conquer my own part of the world...and what I've got is just a business. A successful business, a money-making business most of the time—but it's not great, it's not earth shattering...it's not the dream. And I feel, after all these years, like I've wasted my life and I don't belong there, either.''

Dani closed her fingers around his, aching for him. There had never been a time in her life that Bret's pain was not her own, that his emptiness did not make her feel alone, and she fought against her own helplessness, she strained to make it better for him. Why couldn't he see that *this* was where he belonged? Here, at home, with her?

It came to her so naturally, so totally without surprise, that it was a moment before Dani fully realized the significance of what she felt. And then, on the very heels of that revelation came another, more startling thought. *I'm not sure I love Todd anymore... or that I ever really did.*

She felt disoriented for a moment, shaken to the core, afraid to examine too closely what was slowly being revealed to her. Hesitantly, she unwound her fingers from Bret's and found herself suddenly unable to look at him. But she had to say the rest. There had been too many secrets between them already.

''Bret,'' she said, and she made herself meet his eyes. Her cheeks felt uncomfortably warm. ''There was another reason I yelled at you this afternoon. I think you know what it was.''

He didn't drop his gaze. She loved him for that.

"It was—it was awkward seeing you again after last night," she managed with difficulty. "And I guess— well, you know how I am when I'm uncomfortable. I'm not used to it, I guess, and I get irritable. More angry with myself than with anybody else."

"I know," he said softly. "I felt the same way."

The gratitude in her eyes turned to anxiety as she said in a rush, "Bret, I don't want you to think badly of me. That I—well, that I'm a tramp or—"

His hand seized hers. "I don't think that. I don't want to hear you say that."

"Or," she said, making herself finish with difficulty, "that I was using you. Because—"

His fingers tightened. "Don't," he said huskily. "I know."

She saw the quiet urgency of conviction in his eyes, and it seemed in that moment that he did know, that he knew too much and understood too well, and that the sum of it was something she did not want to hear right now or even to think about.

She dropped her eyes and made herself withdraw her hand again. The next words seemed very difficult to say, and her voice was hoarse with anxiety. "So, is everything all right between us, then?"

He smiled. "Everything's always all right with us, Dani."

After a moment, she returned his smile and stood up.

She was almost to the door when he said, "Dani."

Her heart skipped a beat, and she turned. His face was sober and for a moment, she was certain she saw something forming in his eyes—a question, a statement.... And then it was gone.

He merely smiled again, and said, "Thanks for the cookies."

It was a moment before she could catch her breath, and then she wasn't sure whether it was relief she felt, or enormous, overwhelming disappointment. She nodded, but her throat was too tight to speak. She opened the door and left him alone.

Chapter Nine

"Dani, this is ridiculous," Bret said, pulling up the suspenders of the red felt pants. "I feel like an idiot."

"You look adorable," Dani assured him, handing him the heavily padded red jacket. But even she had trouble repressing a grin. "Tall, skinny Santas are in vogue, everyone knows that. It's the fitness craze."

The schoolroom was empty except for the two of them, but the sounds of revelry from the last-day-of-school Christmas party in the cafeteria drifted down the hall to them. Bret, who had thought Dani's last-minute invitation to join her for the school holiday party would involve nothing more strenuous than drinking green Kool-Aid and eating sugar cookies, eyed the fuzzy white beard and wig skeptically. "Who usually gets to do the honors?"

"Sometimes Dad, sometimes Principal Hollyfield." She tried to hook the beard over his ears but he squirmed away.

"And?"

"And Mr. Hollyfield has the flu, and Dad's working on your house."

Bret, too, had spent a great deal of his time working on the house over the past week, replacing shingles, reinforcing banisters, building steps. It was good, solid, muscle-straining work, and there was an indefinable sense of satisfaction at the end of the day to step back and be able to see the tangible results of what he had done, along with a certain sense of pride to realize that he had not forgotten, in all these years of desk work, the skills that Harold Griffin had taught him in his youth. It was good, too, to see George Skinner out there working and feeling good about his work, for although he wasn't the most skilled carpenter on the job, he was inexhaustible and had a perfectionist's pride that wouldn't let him walk away from any job until it was done right. Bret kept thinking how unfair it was that a man like that couldn't find work, and he found himself wishing there was something more he could do.

When—or if—the electronics plant was built, hundreds of jobs would be created and a lot of problems would be solved for a lot of people, but Bret didn't kid himself that any help would be forthcoming from that quarter for men like Skinner. It could be years before any hiring was done at all, and the best George was qualified for was janitor or night watchman—the latter position fast becoming obsolete, thanks to firms like Underwood Security.

Speculation had been rampant about the electronics plant over the past week. Bret had met Bill Lars, Inushu's forward representative—who was not Japanese at all, but thoroughly west-side Chicago—briefly, just long enough to be cordial, for the project was far too early in development to call for any serious input from Bret at all. But from other sources—Todd, mostly—he had learned Lars had met with town councilmen, county officials and representatives from the utility companies. Apparently, Inushu was very serious, indeed, about making a move, and everyone in town had an opinion on the proposed project. There were times when Bret was reluctant to walk down the street for fear of being assaulted by yet another well-meaning citizen with strong advice—pro or con—on what he should do with his daddy's land. But Dani had not said another word.

Bret got the beard on, and the wig, and topped the costume off with the droopy fur-trimmed hat. He said morosely, "How do I look?"

Dani stepped back, covering her mouth with a curled hand, her eyes twinkling madly. "Like a pregnant track star."

"That does it." Bret grabbed for the hat.

"No, Bret, stop it." She moved forward quickly, laughing, and reached up to straighten his hat. "All you need to do is fix your beard and keep your hat on straight...."

She was leaning against him, reaching up to rearrange the costume hat and beard, her eyes bright with laughter and her face flushed. It was one of those moments that caught them both off guard. The touch, the nearness, the warm sweet fragrance of her perfume... And then she said, perhaps a bit too brightly, "There. Perfect."

She stepped away quickly, bumping the corner of her desk. The movement tipped over a dried out plant, that Bret hastily righted. "What happened to your flower?" he asked.

"It's not a flower," she said, "it's a Christmas cactus. Don't you remember? You sent it to me five years ago."

He examined the plant in his hands uncertainly. "Well, I hope it was in better shape then. Honey, I don't know how to tell you this, but this thing is dead."

"It is not." She took the plant from him firmly and replaced it on her desk. "You sound like Jimmy Skinner. It's supposed to look that way, but it always blooms before Christmas."

"I don't think so." He cast the plant another skeptical look. "Not this year. You'd better throw it out."

"I will not! Do you think I'd throw away something you gave me? It'll bloom. You wait and see. Christmas is just a little slow in coming this year, that's all."

Bret could not repress a grin of familiar, unmitigated affection. "You never change. Hope springs eternal, huh?"

"Right," she replied with a decisive nod. "Now, let's get this show on the road." She picked up the lumpy red sack that matched the costume. "All you have to do is a few ho-ho-ho's and hand out the presents. The kids drew names and put their presents under the tree. The ones in the bag are just little things from the teachers. So every child should get two presents."

"Well, some of them might get three." Bret reached under the desk and pulled out a big box filled with wrapped gifts, and began to transfer them to the Santa sack. "When you mentioned the party," he explained, looking a little abashed, "I thought it wouldn't hurt to get the kids in your class a little something—since I knew them and everything."

She tightened her lips in mock reprimand, her eyes sparkling. "What would Scrooge say?"

He looked up at her. "What did your dad say when you told him he wouldn't be playing Santa this year?"

Dani simply smiled. "He agreed with me—it was about time you got into the Christmas spirit. Are you there yet?"

Bret stood up, hoisted the sack over his shoulder, and replied deadpan, "Ho-ho-ho."

THE SCENE IN THE cafeteria was utter mayhem: the noise level almost at the pain threshold; children, wrapping paper, cookies and punch everywhere. Dani stayed close to Bret, partly to help keep the gift-dispersement going in an orderly fashion, mostly because she was afraid if she didn't stay within grabbing distance, he would run away.

But he surprised her. He made a comical, sometimes satirical Santa Claus, but he threw himself into the part wholeheartedly, booming out his voice to be heard over the clatter, taking little girls on his knee, throwing in a generous sprinkling of ho-ho-hos for effect. Though he did his best to disguise it, there were times when Dani thought he might actually be having fun.

When Jimmy Skinner's name was called, Bret went through his usual routine. "And what do you want for Christmas young man?" he demanded boisterously.

The boy looked at him in disgust. "You're not Santa."

Bret played along. "Now, what makes you say that?"

Jimmy lifted his hand to pull at the beard, but Bret blocked his move with his arm. "Touch the beard and die, kid," he said.

"Santa!" Dani hissed, but she could see a grin tugging at Jimmy's lips.

"There ain't no Santa Claus," Jimmy declared, rocking back on his heels. "And even if there was, you ain't him. Give me my present."

Bret lifted the gaily wrapped package of Christmas candy out of Jimmy's reach. "What do you want for Christmas?" he repeated.

A shadow crossed Jimmy's face that was painful to see on one so young. He mumbled, "Nothing you can give me."

Dani started to intervene, but Bret insisted gently, "Give it a try." Dani held back, watching Jimmy's face.

Jimmy looked at Bret defiantly. "I know who you are. You're fixing up our house. You feel sorry for us, I guess. That's what Daddy says. But it don't make no difference. Nobody's gonna be living there after Christmas. They think I don't know, but I do." He stuck out his hand, his jaw set belligerently, and Dani was alarmed to see the glitter of tears in the boy's eyes.

Bret placed the candy in his hand, and Jimmy turned away.

"Hey, kid." Bret's voice was gruff.

Jimmy turned around and Bret reached into his sack, digging out another present. "Merry Christmas," he said.

Dani placed her hand on Bret's shoulder, and they both watched as Jimmy took his presents across the room, squatted down on the floor and tore the wrapping paper off the biggest one. It was a model airplane. There was wonder in his eyes as he looked back at Bret.

Dani forced a smile, her fingers automatically massaging the tight muscles at the back of Bret's neck. "That was nice," she said softly. "Probably the best present he'll get all Christmas."

Bret shook his head slowly. "I think we both know what that boy wants for Christmas. And he's right, I can't give it to him."

Dani heard the bleakness in Bret's voice, she saw the sorrow and frustration on his face, and she knew what he was feeling because she felt it, too. And she also knew something else, suddenly, simply and without any fanfare at all: that she loved him, more than she had ever loved anyone in her life.

And it really was no surprise; she did not know why she had been fighting it for so long. Hadn't she known, after all, since she was three years old?

She squeezed his shoulder briefly, filled with a quiet and overwhelming joy that needed no words, no further expression. Soon, she knew, the joy would fade and the doubts would surface, the problems would assail her, the complexities and impossibilities would leave her wracked and torn and filled with loss. But for now, she had this happiness inside her, this secret truth, and she wanted to savor it.

"Back to work, Santa," she said, handing Bret another wrapped package. She felt so full of wonder that she was sure he could see it shining softly in her eyes. "Only twenty-five names to go."

TELL HIM, THE LITTLE voice inside Dani kept whispering. *Tell him.*

A light snow was falling through the darkness as they walked across the school parking lot. Bret carried a box filled with the small gifts Dani's students had given her that afternoon—dusting powder, brooches shaped like little birds or Christmas wreaths, hand lotion, little plaques emblazoned "Teacher," pocket handkerchiefs, and the usual assortment of odds and ends—and Dani carried the dried-up Christmas cactus.

"No wonder you like Christmas so much," Bret commented. "You make out like a bandit."

She chuckled. "It makes up for the salary." She glanced at him, wondering if anyone had ever looked so handsome, so strong, so wonderfully familiar and so completely hers. Snow dusted the shoulders of his coat and glistened in his hair under the streetlights. His face was easy and relaxed in profile, tilted upward a little to catch the flakes of snow. Dani found it suddenly impossible to remember a time when he had not been beside her, or to imagine a time when he would not be again.

"I must say," she commented, "you've been an awfully good sport today."

Neither of them had gone home after the school party. It had taken an hour after the last child had gone home for the teachers and staff to clean up the cafeteria, and then it was time to start setting up scenery for the Christmas pageant that night. The children had started arriving for dress rehearsal just as Dani, Bret and several of the teachers returned from having a quick sandwich at the diner across the street, and the past two hours had been an insane whirl of lambs and little ponies, Christmas angels, shepherds and wise men. The children had been stricken with everything from hyperactivity to amnesia. The parents had broken into several spontaneous standing ovations. And Dani, if she had had any sense at all, would have been exhausted. But she wasn't. She was euphoric.

Bret balanced the box on the snow-frosted trunk of Dani's car as she searched for her keys. "At the risk of ruining my image," he admitted, "it was kind of fun. Like walking through a time portal and losing twenty years." And then he smiled at her a little ruefully. "It's like that every time I'm with you. I think you do it on purpose."

"I do," she replied, turning the key in the lock. "My Christmas gift to you—your childhood."

She straightened up, and found that he was still smiling at her. Her heart started beating faster as the little voice insisted again, *Tell him. Tell him now, in the snow with the Christmas lights twinkling in the back-*

ground, while he's close enough to touch and wanting you to touch.... Tell him. Just tell him.

How many times had she heard that voice over the years, and how many times had she refused to listen to it? There had always been some reason for keeping silent: embarrassment, uncertainty, fear of change... fear that Bret would not love her back, fear of making a mistake. Once, she had even—almost—written it down when she thought she couldn't stand the secret feelings that were bursting inside her anymore, but Bret had never seen the letter. When she looked back over the years, it seemed she had made a career out of falling in and out of love with Bret. And it was only now that she realized she had never fallen out of love with him at all.

So why couldn't she tell him now? Tell him that the sister he thought he had was not a sister at all, that the friendship he thought he could count on from her had never been friendship at all, but the love of a woman who only wanted him to love her back...like so many women who had gone before her in Bret's life. Why? There were a thousand old reasons, and almost as many new ones. Because a love affair, once ended, was gone forever. Because she couldn't have stood it if the warmth in Bret's eyes should turn to awkwardness and embarrassment, or even disappointment. Because she had always known it had to come from him because she was frightened and unsure, and she had already risked losing him once when she had kissed him.

Because she already had a man who loved her, who wanted to marry her, who would make a perfect home for her. Because her future was settled and secure and because Bret had always accused her of being a sucker for fantasy, especially at Christmastime. Because she had never done anything impulsive in her life and because, quite simply, she was afraid.

So with her heart beating far too fast and the words she couldn't say choking up her throat, she looked at Bret, and she said instead, simply, "Bret, why don't you stay?"

He looked surprised and then puzzled. "Do you mean...here?" He glanced around. "In Clayville? Forever?"

She could only nod.

She cursed the darkness that disguised his expression from her, the eyes that she could read so well. Because when he returned his gaze to her, all she could make out clearly was the puzzlement, as he replied, "Why would you want me to?"

"There you are!"

A voice behind them made them both turn and the moment for answers and all that hung in the balance with it was gone. Todd lifted his hand to them as he made his way across the crunchy snow.

"Great show, madame producer," he said, dropping his arm around Dani's shoulders. "As usual, I might add."

Dani forced a light laugh as Bret opened the trunk and put the box inside. "Thank you, kind sir. I assume I can look forward to a stellar review in tomorrow's paper?"

"The presses are rolling as we speak." Todd looked at Bret. "We're on our way for a cup of coffee," he said. "Will you join us?"

Bret took the cactus from Dani and locked it in the trunk with the box. "Thanks," he replied with an easy grin, "but this sounds like one of those two's-company situations. Guess I'll go on home and stretch out in front of the fire. I think I heard something about popcorn later."

Dani started to protest, but when Todd said nothing, she hardly could. So she just smiled. "Good night, then. And thanks for all your help."

"Be careful coming home. The roads look slick."

Dani walked across the parking lot with Todd, leaning into the shelter of his arm for balance in the slippery spots, and she could feel Bret watching them. As they moved into the shadow of the building, Todd turned her toward him and kissed her gently, and all Dani could think about was whether or not Bret was still watching.

She knew then why she couldn't tell him. And it broke her heart.

Chapter Ten

Over the next week, Bret was plunged into such a frenzy of Christmas gaiety that he couldn't help but suspect a conspiracy. He was recruited to help collect canned goods for the poor, make Christmas wreaths for the hospital and distribute fruit baskets at the nursing home. People he hadn't seen in twenty years and whose names he barely remembered invited him to Christmas parties and skating parties and hay rides. And behind every face, every invitation, every gaily decorated door and tinkling silver bell, there seemed to be the unspoken questions *See, isn't this what you want? Isn't this what you miss? Isn't this worth preserving? Bret, don't you want to come home?*

He accepted the invitations, he decorated the wreaths, he wrapped big packing crates in foil paper as collection centers, because he was as helpless as anyone else under the Christmas spell and because he knew, deep in his heart, that this might be his last chance. He had been briefly privileged to visit a way of life that had been arrested in time, to return to the streets of his childhood, and it was something to be treasured. But it wouldn't come again. Even as he looked, that small-town innocence was dying out and he might well be the instrument of its final destruction.

He ignored, as much as he could, the business with Inushu. People asked him questions, and he could honestly say he didn't know. He didn't want to know the whens, wheres or hows of the deal, or even how great was the possibility that there would be a deal at all. He was having enough trouble answering his own essential question: Why?

A week ago, the answer had been obvious. Business was business, and if there was one thing he was good at, it was that. But a week ago, Dani hadn't looked up at him through the drifting snow with eyes that were big with unspoken yearning and demanded simply, "Bret, why don't you stay?"

Why don't you stay? His head had reeled with the implications of that question for an hour or more. And it wasn't just the words, but what lay behind them. She had wanted to say more, he was sure of it. He could feel the thoughts crackling through the cold night air like a half-finished sentence, an unresolved chord. *Why don't you stay and...*

And what? Be an usher at her wedding? Play poker with Todd on Thursday nights and watch her children grow up calling him Uncle Bret? Could he do that? *Could* he?

That was why he was so thoroughly determined to enjoy this Christmas. He knew he would never come home again.

He kept himself so busy during that week that he rarely saw Dani, and never alone. He wouldn't have gone shopping in Centerville with them on Saturday except that Miss Annie begged him to come, for the last thing he wanted to do was be a third wheel with Dani and Todd. But it turned out to be a far more pleasant morning than he had anticipated.

Bret remembered Centerville as a dusty, dying town not much different from Clayville, but it had been transformed into a winter wonderland that could have rivaled any eastern tourist trap. The downtown area had been refinished to resemble a quaint turn-of-the-century village that was European in flavor, with gas street lamps, horse-drawn carriages and hand-painted signs. Pricey boutiques lined every street, Victorian Christmas decorations abounded and all the sales personnel wore nineteenth-century costumes. It was charming, business was booming and Bret was amazed. Todd explained how Centerville's success with the tourist industry had attracted bigger business, the new hotel was at ninety percent capacity and a mall and luxury condominiums were already under development. The contrast between Centerville's prosperity and Clayville's seemed unfair.

After the initial tour of the town, they split up into what Bret dryly referred to as "shopping teams." Bret had always hated shopping, and he still did, but Anne was so cheerful and full of fun, it was hard to be in a sour mood. With Anne Griffin as his guide, he bought a new power saw for Harold, which was the only thing he had indicated he would like to have. Then, Bret took Anne to the jewelry store, hoping she'd give some hint as to what she would like. She didn't, but he spent a long time looking at bracelets and charms until he found just what he wanted for Dani—a small, silver bell.

Anne took Bret with her to pick up the coat she had put on layaway for Dani. "I know it's awfully expensive," she confessed, her face glowing as the clerk brought out the russet-colored wool with its soft, white, fur collar. "And this hasn't been our best year at the store, but Dani will never buy a nice coat for herself, and won't it be beautiful on her?"

Anne's own coat had seen many a better day, and impulsively, Bret put his arm around her, hugging her. "You know something, Miss Annie?" he said. "I love you."

And he wondered why it should be so hard to say those same words to her daughter.

Anne looked up at him, laughing. "Why, we love you too, Bret. Now, tell me, what do you want for Christmas?"

All he could think of was Jimmy Skinner's words. *Nothing you can buy me. Nothing anyone can buy me.* But he forced a smile and said, "Surprise me."

At eleven o'clock, they met up with Todd and Dani outside the china shop. "Okay," Dani declared, "now it's boys against the girls." Shifting half her packages into Bret's arms and the other half into Todd's, Dani was just as bright-eyed and as energetic as she had been when she started out two hours earlier. "We'll meet you for lunch at one, in the café across the street. Mom, I want to show you what I found in the window of Odds and Ends...."

Todd and Bret, each loaded down with the women's purchases, watched Dani and Anne hurry off, then looked at each other. Without another word, they crossed the street and took a booth in the café.

"And we call them the weaker sex," Todd commented, groaning a little as he stretched out his legs.

Bret rested his arm along the back of the booth, agreeing, "I think I've had enough Christmas to last me three or four years."

It was quiet inside the restaurant, too early for regular diners, and they had taken a booth by the window so that they could watch for the arrival of the women. Christmas music played softly in the background, and Bret smiled when he recognized "Carol of the Bells."

"That song always reminds me of Dani," he said.

"That's Dani's favorite song," Todd said at the same time.

The moment between them was a little awkward, and then the waitress came to take their order. They both asked for coffee, black.

"This place is pretty impressive," Bret said when the coffee arrived. "Dani said you had something similar in mind for Clayville."

Todd shrugged. "Not the motif, but the idea. Tourist attractions work best in clusters. With Centerville already attracting a lot of traffic, particularly this time of year, there ought to be some way we could capitalize on it. But we haven't even been able to come up with an idea we can all agree on yet, much less starting to put it into practice."

"Put Dani on the town council," Bret suggested lightly, "she'd turn it into a Christmas village."

"Actually, that's not such a bad idea, and we've talked about it. I don't guess I'd be accused of over-stating it if I point out there's a lot of money in Christmas. The trouble is, there's no one on the council—in the whole town, really—who has the kind of experience or expertise it would take to put a plan like that into action. Or any kind of plan."

Bret nodded, sipping his coffee. "Well, the first thing you'd have to do is look into alternative financing. Take this place, for example—it all didn't just spring up full grown and polished overnight. Some-body had to pay to refurbish all these buildings, redo the streets, conceal the wiring.... There are govern-ment programs, of course, and you could offer the business owners incentives, but what I think I'd do is try a lease-back plan—have the city buy whole blocks of downtown property and lease the commercial spaces back to the business operators. That way, you'd have a built-in quality-control system. Of course, that would just be the tip of the iceberg," he went on, warming to the idea. "You'd have to set up a stan-dards-and-practices committee and a financial over-seer, but you'd be amazed at how much funding is available for landmark buildings, and there are defi-nite tax advantages. Of course, what you'd really need is a program administrator to carry something like that through."

Todd was smiling at him so complacently that Bret knew he had been trapped. He dropped his gaze to his cup. "Of course," he said in a much more subdued tone, "none of that is really my field."

"No," agreed Todd. "But it's too bad we don't have a few men like you on the council, who aren't afraid of change and know how to get things done. Then again—" Todd lifted his cup "—it'll all be academic if your sale goes through."

Bret very wisely said nothing.

"Do you know," Todd said after a moment, "I like you. Pretty amazing when you consider how hard I worked at disliking you before I ever met you."

Bret tried not to show his surprise, but Todd just smiled. "Sometimes, I wish you would stay. Like I said, the town needs you. You have a lot of friends in Clayville. All things being equal, I'd probably be one of them eventually. But there's just one problem, isn't there? Dani."

Bret held his silence, but his hand involuntarily tightened on the coffee cup. Todd's gaze wandered casually around the room.

"I knew you'd be trouble," he went on. "I've got to tell you, I got sick of hearing your name this past year, and when I heard you were in town, it was kind of a relief. I figured it would be over, whatever mystique Dani had built up around you, or at the very least, I'd discover your fatal flaw and expose you for the lowlife you had to be...but, of course, that couldn't happen. And you know why, don't you? Dani picked in us carbon copies of each other. We can't dislike each other, and Dani can't choose between us."

Bret thought he could find it very easy in that moment to dislike Todd...except that he knew the man was speaking the truth. He knew it, and he hated the easy, nonchalant way in which Todd declared it. But

Bret couldn't deny it. The only thing he was sure of, suddenly and fiercely, was that he did not want Dani to marry Todd. And it didn't matter that he couldn't think of a good reason why.

Todd brought his gaze back to Bret, and his tone was quiet and sober. "So here's the deal," he said. "I'm thirty-five years old, and I've spent a lifetime preparing to be the kind of husband Dani needs. I know I would be good for her. She's already good for me, better than I can tell you. I've loved her from the first minute I met her, but I guess you know how easy that is. All I want is her happiness, and I've never been able to say that about any other person I've ever known. So what I want to know now is this—do you love her enough to let her go?"

And there it was. Clear, simple and out in the open. What Bret had been avoiding trying to say to himself since he had come back; the reason, ultimately that he had come back: if he lost Dani now, it would be forever. If he let her go, there would be no second chance. She would marry another man, and that man would be good for her, he would make her happy, he would give her everything she needed. How could Bret keep her from doing what was best for her, the only possible choice she could make? If he loved her, why would he even want to?

But how could he let her go?

He met Todd's eyes, and he responded softly, "Do you?"

For a long moment, the two men looked at each other; stalemate. Then Todd glanced at his watch.

"Well," he said, "I still have a few things to pick up. Will you watch the packages?"

Bret picked up his coffee cup. "Yeah. No problem."

Todd stood up and looked down at Bret for a moment. "So," he said. His voice had a note of finality in it, but no hostility. It was simply a matter of lines being drawn. "I guess there's nothing more to say except... may the best man win."

The bell over the door clanged as Todd left, and Bret sank back against the booth, staring into his coffee. "Yeah," he murmured. "That's what I'm afraid of."

"Look, Mom." Dani flipped excitedly through the pages of a book. "*The History and Settlement of Calvin County.* It's got Zac and Hannah's story in it."

Her mother looked appreciatively over Dani's shoulder at the chapter headings. "I'm going to get this for Bret," she decided. "He's always half accused me of making that story up."

Her mother smiled. "Bret has never been as sentimental as you are."

The excitement faded from Dani's face, and her eyes grew thoughtful, even a little sad, as she agreed, "No. I guess not." But she took the book to the counter and asked to have it gift wrapped.

"He's a hard man to buy for," her mother went on as they waited. "I thought about a nice sweater—the poor boy doesn't seem to own anything but jeans and T-shirts—but then, I suppose that wouldn't do him much good in California, would it?"

Inexplicably, Dani felt her throat tighten. "Maybe he won't go back to California," she said.

"Of course, he will." Anne sounded surprised. "Is there any reason he shouldn't?"

Unexpectedly and totally unpreventably, Dani's eyes flashed with tears. She didn't know why, and if she had had even a moment's notice, she certainly would have been able to prevent them. But with her mother's plain, matter-of-fact words, it was as though all the strain, the secrecy, the yearning of the past week combined into one searing stab of hopelessness; her throat burned and her eyes filmed and the truth was like a leaden weight settling in her stomach.

She turned away quickly, but not before Anne's eyes softened with sympathy and concern and gentle understanding that tore at Dani's conscience like shredded glass. She paid for her purchase blindly and left the bookstore.

Her mother gestured to a bench just outside the store, and Dani followed her there without protest. They sat in silence for a time while Dani struggled to regain control of herself. The laughing shoppers, the gay decorations, the tinkle of bells from sidewalk Santas all faded into a blur, and Anne covered Dani's gloved hand with her own. "Honey, what are you going to do?" she asked tenderly.

Dani swallowed hard, hardly trusting herself for speech, unable to look at her mother. "Oh, Mom, I feel so bad. Todd is so wonderful, and I can't hurt him. I thought we had a future together, I really did, and you know I've had a crush on Bret since I was—

was a kid—'' Here her voice broke, and her mother patted her hand.

"Does Bret know?"

Dani shook her head mutely, tightening her jaw against the tears that surged and receded and surged again.

Anne was silent for a time, and then she said, "You're right. Todd is a wonderful man. He's all your father and I ever could have wanted for you, and the two of you make a beautiful couple. I know that he adores you. But it's more than a crush you feel for Bret, isn't it?"

Dani looked at her mother, miserable and helpless. "Yes," she whispered. "And it's been going on so long that I—I hardly realized when he stopped being my friend and started being the only man I've ever loved.... But he doesn't feel the same way about me, and even if he did, he would never tell me because..."

Anne nodded. "Because of Todd."

"And other things." Dani looked down at the sidewalk, blotting her eyes with the back of her coat sleeve.

"Bret's an honorable man," Anne said. "And sensible."

Dani looked up at her, pleading. "Mom, do you think it's wrong the way I feel? What should I do?"

Her mother smiled, tiredly it seemed, and slipped her arm around Dani's shoulders, drawing her close in a gentle embrace. "No, darling," she said. "I don't think it's wrong. I think it's...inevitable. As for what you should do, I wish I could tell you. I really do."

She leaned away and took Dani's chin in her hand, looking into her eyes as though she could impart courage with her smile. "You'll make the right choice, Dani," she said. "But you have to make it alone."

"It's scary," Dani whispered.

Anne sighed as she drew Dani's head onto her shoulder again. "I know, baby," she said softly, "I know."

But that was of no help at all.

BRET HELPED THE WOMEN carry their packages inside, then made himself scarce as they went upstairs to giggle and whisper over their purchases. He himself had come away with a down-filled parka for Miss Annie in addition to the power saw he'd bought for her husband, and, on an impulse, he'd purchased a whimsical coffee mug with a cartoon-character cat exclaiming "Bah, Humbug!" for his secretary. That one he had already had the store ship; he hoped to persuade Dani to wrap the others...except, of course, for the bracelet he'd gotten her. That one he wanted to wrap himself.

He was in the kitchen, making a pot of coffee, when the phone rang. "I'll get it!" he called upstairs.

Miss Annie's voice floated down to him. "Thanks, Bret."

He was surprised when the voice on the other end asked for him. "Speaking."

"One moment, please. Mr. Notions is calling."

The secretary transferred the call and in record time, Craig's voice boomed over the line. "Well, young man, you must have been a very, very good boy this year."

Then tension that went through every fiber of Bret's body was as sharp as a headache. "Don't play games, Craig."

"All right, short and sweet. Inushu is ready to make an offer."

Bret's voice was flat. "How much?"

"Well, I don't want to jinx it, but let's just say I threw out a figure roughly the equivalent of twice the appraised value and they didn't blink an eye."

Bret sank back against the wall. His throat was dry, and his fingers were tight on the receiver. He tried very hard to make his mind blank.

"Now, the project developer wants to go over the site personally, so what do you say to next Wednesday? We'll be coming in by private plane, so let's say ten o'clock at the property."

Bret cleared his throat. "Umm, I don't known. There's someone living in the house...."

"What house? Nobody cares about houses. It's just a formality. The guy wants to see what he's getting. Nobody has to even know we're there. Ten o'clock Wednesday, and be ready to sign on the dotted line."

"Right. Sure, Craig, sounds fine." Bret gathered his scattered thoughts long enough to inquire, "So that's it, then? It's really a go?"

"All that's missing is the signatures. And don't bother to thank me. All part of the job."

Bret managed a dry smile. "And the commission."

"Well, there's always that. Wednesday, then. I'll call if there's a change."

"Thanks, Craig."

For a long time after he'd replaced the receiver, Bret stood there, leaning against the wall, trying to take it all in. He had done it. He had come here to sell the property and, as though it were a special-order miracle, he had sold it. Not only had he sold it, but in a way that would change the face of this town forever, and it was a good thing. The *best* thing.

The view through the window was of another leaden day, and he could hear the rhythmic sound of an ax as Harold split kindling for the fireplace. *Wood splitter,* Bret thought absently. *That's what I should've gotten him.* But somehow, he didn't think that was a gift that would be greatly appreciated. Harold was a man who liked to do things the old-fashioned way. A wood splitter would be as out of place around here as . . . as an electronics plant.

Bret did not know how long Dani had been standing at the door before he sensed her presence, but from the expression on her face, he knew it had been long enough to overhear at least part of the telephone conversation. He forced a smile and gestured toward the telephone.

"My real-estate agent," he explained. "Maybe you gathered."

Her voice was cautious. "You have an offer?"

"A whopper." He went over to the coffeepot, straining for enthusiasm he didn't feel. "Sounds like they want to finalize the deal as early as Wednesday, can you believe that?" He took a mug off the rack. "Coffee?"

Dani crossed the room, moving as if the floor were strewn with booby traps. "So they're serious, then. This could really happen."

"It *has* happened." He abandoned the effort at bright spirits and let his voice fall flat as he filled his cup. Then he turned to her, bracing himself. "I guess a lot of people around here are going to be pretty upset with me." *Including you,* he thought. *Mostly you.*

But she kept her emotions very tightly disguised, even though her voice was beginning to show the strain. "Just because they made an offer doesn't mean you have to accept."

His laugh was short and devoid of mirth. "You haven't heard the offer yet."

"So what did they do?" she shot back, and the careful dance around emotions they had been doing was completely abandoned. "Threaten to break your knees? Put a dead horse's head in your bed? Come on, Bret, you're not that greedy! You've lived without their money for years, the world's not going to come to an end if you don't take it now!"

"It's not greed!" Tension knotted in his muscles again, and though he tried to keep his voice calm, he did not succeed very well. "It's good business, but it's more than that. Damn it, Dani, let's not start this again. This is progress. It's good for the town—it may be the only chance this town has. Why do you keep trying to make me out to be the bad guy?"

"You're not doing this for the town!" she cried. "You're not even doing it for you—because you need the money or because it's good business or anything else! You're doing it because you can't stand to see anything stay static, because you want to put as much distance between you and the past as you can, and if you have to destroy the past to do it, then that's okay, too, isn't it?''

"That's not true," he said hoarsely.

But she shook her head violently, her ponytail lashing across her face with a gesture that was swift and abrupt, as though she were trying to shake off the aura of him or rid herself of a bad taste. "You couldn't wait to get out of here when you were a kid, you couldn't get far enough away—"

"For God's sake, Dani, that was college!"

"You never came back. You didn't even think about it—"

"I came back!"

"You never *cared* about things the way I do!" she cried. "I always thought you did, but I was wrong. All these years, I've been wrong about you."

"I cared," he said fiercely. His hand was wound so tightly around the coffee cup that his fingers hurt. "I've always cared." And suddenly, he realized he was not talking about the land or his hometown or any of the things from his past...or perhaps he was. Perhaps, all of those things and Dani were inextricably mixed. He only knew that when he looked at her, the hurt and the disappointment in her eyes went through him like the slow-cutting edge of a dull knife and an emptiness filled him that was bigger than any defeat he had ever known.

He said quietly, tiredly, "We were always different, Dani. I guess the only thing we ever had in common was each other."

Her eyes were big and far too bright. He saw her raise her hand to her throat as though it hurt her. He turned away, looking out the window, focusing his gaze on the trampled, churned up snow, the stark silhouette of an ice-glazed tree at the turn of the drive. The silence pulsed between them, heavy and desolate.

After a moment, he murmured, "Footprints in the snow."

"What?" Her voice was hoarse, confused.

He did not turn around. If he saw tears in her eyes now, even tears of anger, he would not be able to stand it. "Zac and Hannah. I always wondered why they didn't just follow those footprints in the snow."

"Maybe..." She drew in a soft, unsteady breath. "Maybe they were afraid."

"Maybe."

She said softly, "Are you afraid, Bret?"

He could feel her eyes on him, as gentle as a questing caress, as hesitant as a whisper. His muscles tensed against it, he made himself stand still. Afraid? Oh, yes. Afraid of making another mistake, afraid of hurting Dani, afraid of being wrong...maybe just afraid of being happy.

He glanced down, surprised to find the coffee cup still in his hand. Though he didn't want it, he took a sip. And he kept his gaze fixed on the view through the window. "When I was a kid," he said, "it was all so simple. There was so much to do, so much to explore. I didn't find what I expected to, and maybe now, it doesn't seem as important as it once did, but somebody once said the only thing worse than wanting and not having is not knowing what you want."

Her voice was tight and strained behind him, but strangely low, with a husky, seductive quality that reverberated in his blood. "You know what you want, Bret. You're just afraid to ask for it."

He drew in his breath but couldn't release it. His chest was tight, and his blood was racing. He felt disoriented; he wasn't sure what they were talking about anymore. Because he did know what he wanted and he would never, ever ask for it.

Dani moved forward. She reached out her hand to touch his arm, but let it drop. Bret looked at her and saw a jaw that was tightly set, eyes that were wide and unafraid, a face that was filled with all the stubborn, unflinching honesty he had ever loved, and it was with all the will at his command that he refused to reach for her. She said steadily, "You have choices, Bret. You always have choices."

It was as though a line had been drawn through time, separating one moment from the next, what was from what might be, and whatever he said now would change his future—both their futures—forever. There was no shying away from that line; time moved on.

"Yes," he agreed huskily. "I have choices." And then, deliberately, he turned back to the window. "But none of them appeals to me."

He took a sip of the coffee, trying to make the gesture casual, and then he said the words. "I guess I'll be going back to L.A. after I meet with those people Wednesday. I know I said I'd stay for Christmas, but it's really a bad time to be away from the office. All I really came here for was to check out the property, you know." The words tasted like poison on his tongue and he could feel them sting her flesh as though it were his own. "Of course," he added, lifting the cup again, "I'll come back for your wedding."

"My wedding?" The words were repeated blankly, like a recording.

He turned, making himself smile, making it look genuine. "You did mean to invite me, didn't you?"

Her face was as blank as her voice, as though all the life had been drained out of it. Only her eyes remained animated, busily searching, probing his. He withstood the assault manfully. "Of course. Of course, I'll invite you. But I never— I didn't say—"

He deliberately deepened the smile. "Come on, Dani, you've tortured the guy long enough. You know you're going to marry him. Give the poor fellow a break. Say yes."

Still the searching, almost a plea, maybe even a hint of desperation. Bret made himself put the coffee cup on the counter before his tight fingers crushed it.

"Is that what you want me to do?" she said, so softly he almost had to strain to hear.

He shrugged. "What I want doesn't have anything to do with it. But if you want my advice, you're a fool to let this one get away. I know how it feels to be over thirty and alone, Dani, and guys like Todd don't come along every day. Not in this hick burg, anyway."

"No," she whispered. She never took her eyes off him. "They don't."

Her gaze was like a laser, burning away the layers of his defense. Any moment now, she would break through the final thin barrier and discover "lies" written in black letters all over his soul. He couldn't look at her anymore. He couldn't stay here anymore. He couldn't lie to her anymore.

He turned for the door as casually as possible. "I think I'll go give your dad a hand."

"Bret."

He almost made it. He had one hand on his coat, the other on the door. He looked back.

Her face still looked stunned, her eyes ravaged, but her voice was almost normal. "I came down to see if you had anything you wanted me to wrap for you."

It actually hurt to smile, but he managed it. "Thanks. I'll bring them up to your place later."

She nodded, and he left as quickly as he could.

HE HAD DONE THE RIGHT thing. Bret breathed deeply of the sharp, icy air and repeated the assurance to himself in time with the crunch of his footsteps on the snow. He had done the only possible thing.

Do you love her enough to let her go?

He had let her go because he had no choice. Because one of them deserved to be happy and because it had to be Dani. That was all.

The ax was stuck in the chopping block, but Harold Griffin had apparently abandoned the chore. Bret picked up the tool, centered a log and began to swing with a vengeance. He brought the ax up and down, back and forth, taking satisfaction in the thud of each swing, the flying of chips. Sweat filmed his face and chilled him beneath his coat. His hands stung, and more than once, he came very close to losing a foot, but he didn't stop.

Then a mild voice spoke up behind him. "You fixing on killing something, son, or you figure you just need the exercise?"

Bret staggered back, panting, and let the ax drop as he turned to face Harold. He pushed his hair back, waiting for his breath to return, and he could have tossed off some off-hand explanation for his sudden burst of energy. But he was too defeated, too worn out and bruised inside to dissemble. Not again.

He bent and began to gather up the splintered wood. "I got an offer on my property."

The other man's voice was mild. "Good for you."

"It is good," Bret said tightly. "It's good for everybody. Your property values will go sky high."

"Yeah, I reckon they would, if I had a mind to sell. Which I don't."

"People will be moving in from all over. You won't be able to keep up with the business at your store. And if Todd Renshaw thinks he's got a newspaper now, just wait until he has something to really write about. Circulation will double, just like the population. And with the revenues the county will be bringing in, there'll be plenty to put into the school—they might even build a new one. The teachers can get the supplies they need and—"

"Yep," agreed Harold. "Sounds like it's going to be good for everybody. And two young people couldn't ask for a better wedding gift than the future you've got plotted out for them."

Bret tensed, then straightened up. He couldn't keep the belligerence out of his voice or his pose. "But you don't want an electronics plant in your backyard."

Harold just smiled, adjusting his cap a little more snugly on his head. "I've seen a lot of changes, Bret. I guess I can handle this one."

"I know people are going to accuse me of selling out. There's going to be an uproar, there always is in small towns like this. Shortsightedness, that's the problem. Nobody can accept progress."

"Seems to me you're a lot more upset by this than anybody I know."

Bret dumped an armload of kindling into the wood box and turned for more.

"Nobody's forcing you to sell, you know," Harold went on. "I've often wondered about it, Bret. Why don't you just come on back home here and settle down?"

"I can't."

"Why not?"

"Because I'm in love with Dani." He hadn't meant to say that; he couldn't believe it when he heard the words leave his mouth. He let the kindling slip from his fingers, and he looked up at Harold, stunned.

But the other man just smiled. "Well," he said mildly, "it's about damn time."

Bret stood up slowly, expecting to feel embarrassed, shocked, apologetic. What he felt was an enormous sense of relief. He had said it, if not to her, then to someone. It was out and he didn't have to hide it anymore. No more lies.

Harold shoved his hands into the pockets of his coat and rocked back slightly on his heels. "We've been expecting this for some time now, you know. About twenty years, I'd say. But let me see if I've got this straight. You're in love with my daughter, so you figure the best thing you can do is the one thing that will make her mad—sell the old homestead. Then I guess you'll go on back to California without her." He nodded. "Makes sense."

Bret drew an arm across his face tiredly. "There's nothing else I can do. Dani's life is here. Mine's on the coast. She's got everything going for her now. I can't just come in and tear it all apart."

"What does Dani have to say about all this?"

"Nothing. I haven't told her."

"I can't say that's the smartest thing I've ever known you to do."

Bret shook his head tersely. "She's in love with Todd."

"Maybe. Maybe not. But she's got a right to know and to make up her own mind."

Just as Bret had had a right to know ten years ago.

He returned Harold's gaze bleakly. "Even if I wanted to stay here, even if Dani wanted me, I couldn't make a living here. There's not a lot of call for burglar alarms and security patrols around here, and I don't know anything else."

"You could always learn."

But Bret shook his head. "I lost one marriage," he said simply. "I can't take a chance with Dani. Besides, it's too late." He looked back toward the house. "I just told Dani I wanted her to marry Todd."

"Maybe she won't listen to you."

Bret managed a smile, though it was weary and sad. "She always listens to me," he said. "That's the trouble."

FROM HIS WINDOW BRET could see Dani's house. There was a light on in the loft, and when he strained, he thought he could see a shadow pass before it, but it turned out to be only a branch moving in the wind.

She's got a right to know....

And she did. She had a right to know the one thing he could never tell her, but if he had to lie to her one more time, the stain would be on his conscience forever. She had a right to know, and he had a right to tell her.

He went over to the small writing desk beside the closet and opened a drawer. Among the odds and ends, he found an old ruled notepad and several ballpoint pens. Bret tore a sheet off the pad and picked up a pen.

Dear Dani,

I know it doesn't make any difference now, but I love you. I love you as a man loves a woman, and I want you like a man wants a woman, and I think I have for years. I wish it could have been different for us, but I only want you to be happy. Please believe that.

Your best friend,

Bret

He looked at the paper for a long time, aching inside, wishing, wondering.... And then he folded the paper, tore it neatly in half, folded it again and tore it again. He opened his hand and watched the pieces drift into the trash can.

Chapter Eleven

Dani had not spent an evening alone with Todd since Bret had come home. She hadn't planned it that way— she was sure she hadn't—but the holidays were always hectic. Tonight, they had been to a party and it was only natural that he should come inside when he took her home. It made Dani a little nervous, for reasons she didn't want to think about.

She hadn't wanted to go to the party, but once there, she had deliberately—somewhat fiercely—set out to have a good time. It was almost as though she was desperately trying to prove she could have a good time without Bret, which was ridiculous because she had had plenty of good times before he had arrived. Hundreds of good times.

"I was surprised Bret wasn't there tonight," Todd commented, helping her off with her coat.

"He doesn't know everyone in town," she replied a bit sharply. And then, forcing a more casual tone, she added, "Besides, I guess it's getting a little awkward for him, explaining about the land deal. He thinks the whole town is going to get up in arms over it." And then, refusing to let the conversation focus on Bret, she said brightly, "Look, there are still a few embers in the fireplace. Think you can get a fire stirred up?"

"At your service." Todd hung his coat on the rack beside hers. "How about something to drink?"

"Wine or coffee? Or I think I've got some eggnog left." Bret's eggnog.

"Wine, I think."

She hurried to the kitchen, and once there, she braced her hands on the counter, taking a deep breath, trying to steady her nerves. But it wasn't just nerves. She felt raw inside, battered, exposed and shaken, and she had felt that way ever since the encounter with Bret the afternoon before. She went through the day, she laughed and she talked and she moved and she kept busy, but she was still in something of a state of shock.

Over and over, she told herself how lucky she was. She had done everything but throw herself at Bret's feet—more than once she had literally thrown herself into his arms. She had given him every possible chance to reciprocate her feelings... but he hadn't. He must have known; there had been a moment yesterday when she was sure he knew, when she felt with every fiber of her being that he was on the verge of telling her the same thing—but he hadn't. He had let the moment slip by, and he had done it so easily, so gracefully, that not even a dent was left in their friendship to show how close she had come to stepping over the line. She should be grateful. She *was* grateful. She had almost made the biggest mistake of her life, and Bret had saved her.

Except that she did not feel as though she'd been saved. She felt lost and numb, and she couldn't explain it.

Bret was right. Men like Todd didn't come along every day and she was lucky, so lucky to have found him. She wanted to get married, to have children and grandchildren and the same man by her side day and night...and Bret did not want her. She had almost thrown it all away for a man who didn't want her, and in so doing, she would have lost twice: Todd, the man who should be her husband, and Bret, her best friend. She was very, very lucky.

She poured the wine and came back into the living room. Todd was sitting on the floor before the fireplace, coaxing a blaze from the logs. He had plugged in the Christmas-tree lights, and the twinkling lights added their play to the glow of the fire that planed his face. Dani felt a rush of tenderness looking at him, and reminded herself again how lucky she was. Suddenly, she wanted to be held, needed to be taken into strong, loving arms and kissed and stroked.

But not by him.

She pushed the treacherous thought out of the way and crossed the room, dropping onto the hearth rug beside him. He took the glass of wine from her, smiling. "Did I tell you how pretty you look tonight?"

"Several times." The party had not been formal and she was wearing winter white wool pants and a bright red overblouse with a floppy bow. She did not feel particularly ravishing, but it was nice to hear Todd say that she was. Nice to know that to some man, somewhere, she would always be beautiful.

Todd said, "So Bret's leaving after he makes the deal Wednesday."

Dani took a sip of her wine. "That's right."

"I've been looking into the Inushu plans. I'm starting to come up with some pretty interesting information."

"I don't want to talk about that," Dani said abruptly.

He looked surprised. "You might want to know what I've found out."

She shook her head. "I don't want to talk about electronics or Japanese or Bret, not tonight. I'm not interested and I don't care, not about any of it."

He smiled. "Well, I've got to say I don't believe you don't care. But it is nice, I'll admit, not to talk about Bret for once."

He lifted his hand, encircling her neck, his expression tender and adoring in the firelight. Dani thought he was going to kiss her. She wanted to kiss him. She was sure she did.

And then he let his hand trail down her arm. He said, "I brought a little something for you to put under your tree." He put down the wineglass and reached into his pocket. "But I think I'd rather have you open it now."

"Oh, Todd, it's too early for presents," she said starting to protest, and then she stopped as he drew out a small, square box wrapped in gold paper.

Dani's heart pounded and her fingers shook a little as she took it from him. She knew what was inside. She knew it by the shape of the box, by the look on his face, by the simple perfection of it all. A Christmas engagement, a New Year's announcement, a spring wedding... Perfect. Just perfect.

Visions of bridal showers, shopping trips, flower girls and white lace were skating through her head as she tore off the gold wrapping and lifted the lid. The small solitaire gleamed like a droplet of ice against the blue velvet, catching the glow of the fire and the spark of the tree lights. All engagement rings should be seen by firelight, she thought. It was perfect.

The ring glowed like a promise there on the velvet, and Todd's hand was warm and loving on her arm. She reached to draw it out and slip it onto her finger. But she couldn't.

The tears burned her eyes, trembling on her lashes. "I'm sorry," she whispered, and closed the lid.

The fire popped, and outside, an icy branch creaked in the wind. The silence between them was long and full and aching. Then Todd smiled a little and said, "Overplayed my hand, huh?"

She swallowed hard and shook her head. He wouldn't take the box from her, so she placed it on the hearth. Then he said one word.

"Bret."

Not a question, but a statement of fact.

Dani stood, hugging her arms, pressing her lips tightly together to stop the tremors, but still, her voice was broken. "Oh, Todd, I've been so unfair to you." She tried to draw a breath, but it sounded more like a sob. "I didn't mean to be, I swear I didn't. I always knew I wasn't sure, but I never knew why until... Still, I wanted to marry you, I wanted to believe we could be happy together, that—that he would go away and everything would be the way it used to be, but it can't be. I know that now. And I can't marry you when I'm in love with another man.''

After a long moment, Todd said, ''Well, thank you for that, at least.''

He stood up slowly, standing very close, but Dani couldn't turn to look at him. She stood with her head lowered, gripping her arms and choking back tears, and after a moment, Todd laid his hand lightly on her shoulder in a comforting, reassuring gesture. ''I had to know, Dani,'' he said. ''I couldn't go on like this. I just had to know.''

She watched as he bent to pick up the jewel box and turned toward the door. Then he stopped. A strangely sad half smile curved his lips as he said, ''You know something? If you would've had me, I think I would have married you anyway.''

Dani squeezed her eyes tightly shut and listened to the sound of his retreating footsteps, to the soft closing of the door. Then she couldn't fight it any longer. She began to sob, and once she started, she couldn't stop. She cried far, far into the night.

BLUE SKIES WERE spilling in through her window when Dani awoke late the next morning. Her eyes were swollen, and her chest felt stuffy, as though she were coming down with a bad cold, but she knew it was only the residue of tears. She had fallen asleep atop the bedspread, exhausted from crying, fully clothed, with only an afghan to keep off the night's chill. She had cried for Todd and for Bret and for herself; she had cried in anger and hopelessness and self-pity and frustration and in sheer, raw pain. Dani rarely cried; in fact, she could not remember a time in her life when she had wept so helplessly and for so long. Surely she had plumbed the depths of human misery.

People said such a catharsis was therapeutic and that things always looked better in the morning. Nothing could have been farther from the truth. The bright winter sunlight mocked the bleakness inside her soul when she opened her eyes, and all she wanted to do was pull the afghan over her head and lie there, numb with despair, until spring.

She should have been relieved it was over. No more lies, no more deception. She had made her choice... and she had lost everything.

She moved her eyes around the room, trying to take comfort in the familiarity of her surroundings. The Christmas cards that Bret had helped her string along the loft railing, the garland that Bret had wound around the bannister, the mistletoe... the Christmas cactus, as withered as her dreams, on her bedside table. But she hadn't lost everything. She still had her home, her family, the friends she loved, the town in which she had grown up.... But even that was changing, slipping away from her, outgrowing her. Soon, there would be nothing left.

She made herself get off the bed, shivering a little as her stockinged feet struck the bare floor. She might feel as though the world had ended, but in truth, life went on and she had plenty to do today. One night of mourning was enough to give to a man who didn't love her and to an engagement that had never been. She refused to wallow in self-pity. She couldn't afford to.

She started for the shower, but on her way, she paused and picked up the cactus. She looked at it for a minute, then dropped it into the trash can. Bret was right. She did have a tendency to hold on to things long past their time...things like hope—and even love. And the plant was as dead as it was ever going to get.

The hot shower restored her body, taking the puffiness out of her eyes and the soreness out of her muscles, but the physical well-being was abrasive, even painful, in contrast to the ache she felt inside. She would have to tell her mother. She'd have to tell a lot of people who would be expecting to see Todd and her together during the holidays, make a lot of excuses, face up to a lot of disappointment...and Bret. Bret would have to know. But she couldn't face him. Someone else would have to tell him, because she couldn't. He would be leaving in a few days anyway, and once he was gone...

Once he was gone, he wouldn't come back. She knew that as clearly as she had ever known anything in her life.

Someone was knocking on her door when she came out of the shower, wrapped in a terry cloth robe and drying her hair with a towel. Her heart started pounding as she gripped the banister. Her parents never knocked. Bret. Or Todd...

She went down the stairs quickly, uncertain whether to feel dread or anticipation, and not fully able to feel either, thinking only, *Not this morning, not now. I can't deal with either of them now....*

But when she opened the door, it was neither of them. A stranger in a postal uniform stood there, smiling at her. "Morning, miss. Package for you." He offered her a medium-size box, with the rest of the mail stacked on top of it.

She stared at him. "You're not the usual mailman. Where's Mr. Redman? He's not sick, is he?"

"Not that I know of." The stranger's blue eyes twinkled with good humor beneath the visor of his cap, and his cheeks were as red as cherries in the cold. A shock of white hair encircled his head beneath the cap in the back, and he looked like a thoroughly pleasant, very cheerful fellow. Dani was just surprised that she didn't recognize him; she knew everyone in town. "I'm just helping out for the holidays."

"Oh." She took the package from him. "I'm sorry you had to come to the door. I've been meaning to get a bigger mailbox."

"No trouble." He tipped his hat to her. "Have a Merry Christmas, now."

"Thank you. You, too."

The package was from Aunt Flora in New Jersey, and even though the box inside was wrapped with an expensive department-store wrapping and prominently displayed a Do Not Open Until Christmas sticker, under other circumstances, Dani wouldn't have been able to resist peeling open a corner and taking a peek. Today, she wasn't interested. She put the package under the tree and flipped through the other envelopes in a desultory fashion. Christmas cards, bills . . . she didn't feel like opening those, either. She tossed the lot on the end table, and then something caught her eye.

It was a plain white envelope, not Christmas-card size, and it didn't have a return address. It didn't, in fact, have any address at all. It was completely blank, front and back, and as Dani examined it curiously, she started toward the door, wondering if the new postman had made a mistake. But she could already hear his Jeep moving down the road, and there was only one way to find out. She opened the envelope and pulled out a single sheet of lined note paper.

Dear Dani,
   I know it doesn't make any difference now...

THE WORDS FROM THE OLD song, "California Dreaming" were going through Bret's head as he crossed the drive toward Dani's house. At another time, the irony of the song would have brought a wry smile to his lips, but today, it simply haunted him, chilling him to his soul. He wasn't dreaming about California. If he dreamed about any place from now on, it would be here, where she was.

One hand was shoved deep into his coat pocket for warmth, in the other, he carried a snow shovel slung over his shoulder. The temperature was supposed to go above freezing today, and Harold had wanted to make sure Dani's porch and drive were cleared of snow before it turned to slush and then refroze into dangerous ice. Bret had volunteered for the job because men Harold's age shouldn't be wielding a snow shovel, and because he knew he couldn't go forever avoiding Dani.

She had gone to a party with Todd last night. He had watched them drive away with a bitterness in his throat and an ache in his heart, then he had turned away from the window and set about being the most cheerful, entertaining and helpful houseguest Harold and Anne Griffin had ever had. It would be hell getting through the next three days, trying to act normal with Dani, trying to give the people he loved memories they could treasure of his last visit home, trying, above all else, not to let any of them know that every minute he stayed here was killing him inside.... And yet, three days was not nearly long enough.

It wasn't long enough to make things right between them. It wasn't long enough to see her laugh again, to hear her joke with him as she used to, to walk with her in the snow, talking about nothing at all, just feeling good being together. It wasn't long enough to see her eyes light up like a child's when she opened her presents on Christmas morning or to go caroling with her or to dance with her in the light of the Christmas tree... because everything was changed now. And he didn't have that magical power of Dani's to turn back time, to erase the years and bring back innocence. He couldn't undo what he had done or take away the memory of the hurt and disappointment in Dani's eyes his words had caused.

He had almost reached her porch and was debating whether to go up and knock or to simply get on with his work when, suddenly, the door flew open and Dani burst out. She was wearing a bath robe, her eyes were blazing as she plunged down the steps toward him.

He dropped the shovel. "Dani, what's wrong!"

"You dirty, rotten, lying *snake!*"

She drew back her arm to strike him, and it was only instinct that caused him to catch her arm, fending off the blow. She struggled, slipping on the snow-packed ground, and the robe parted to give him a glimpse of her naked chest and one slim thigh. "You lied to me!" she shouted at him. Her color was high and her face wild with fury. "All this time you—"

"Are you crazy?" He grabbed her and shook her because he didn't know what else to do. "Running out here in your bathrobe and bare feet—your hair is wet!"

"Let go of me!" She wrenched away violently, her eyes and her face like fire. "How dare you! How *could* you? Do you know what you put me through? Do you have any idea?"

He was becoming angry now himself. "What are you talking about?"

"This!" She raised a closed fist at him and he saw that it concealed some kind of crumpled paper. "Is that it, then? Were you just going to sneak away and forget about me? Was that the plan, never telling me, letting me wonder? You lying, cheating, lowdown son of a—"

"Get in the house, for heaven's sake!" He shoved her toward the door. "You can't stand around half-naked in the snow screaming at me for no good reason—especially not if you're going to use that kind of language!"

"I can scream at you wherever I want!"

"Get inside!"

He grabbed her arm and half pushed her up the steps, slamming the door behind him with a little more force than necessary when they were inside. "Now what in God's name is this all about?"

"This!"

She shoved the paper at him again, and this time he snatched it from her, scowling as he unfolded it. "Get something on your feet," he commanded her shortly. "You're going to catch cold."

But then the words on the paper leapt up at him. His words. His paper. His handwriting. He could feel the blood drain from his face, but he couldn't tear his eyes away from the writing. "Where did you get this?" he demanded hoarsely.

"What does it matter where I got it? Did you leave it in my mailbox? Were you just going to walk away and leave that for goodbye? Or were you going to mail it from California? Damn you, Bret, why couldn't you just *tell* me?"

He looked up at her, numbed beyond all feeling. "I tore it up. It was a secret, like we used to—"

"A secret!" Her voice had gone from righteous outrage to despair. "For the love of heaven, don't you know what I've been going through these past weeks? Why would you want to keep it a *secret?*"

"I tore it up..." he repeated dully. "I threw it away..." But there were no tears in the letter, no tape, not even any creases, except the ones Dani had made with her angry fist.

"Oh, Bret, I've been in love with you most of my life! When we were teenagers, when you went away to college, even when you came back—to tell me you were getting married..." Her voice broke, and was a note lower in pitch as she continued. "Oh, God, I did everything but *beg* you to love me back! And these last weeks—you *knew* what was happening between us, you knew how I felt, and yet you—"

"You shouldn't have this," he said, looking at the paper. "There is no way you could have this."

"Bret, are you listening to me?" she cried. "Have you heard one word I've said? I love you!"

And then he did hear her, or he thought he did. The words drifted to him as though through a heavy fog, and he looked up at her, feeling numb, disbelieving, a little drugged. "What?" he said hoarsely. "What did you say?"

She stood less than three feet away from him, her cheeks stained with color and her eyes defiant, her chin lifted coolly. "I said," she repeated deliberately, "that I'm in love with you. I said you're a fool for not realizing it before and doing something about it. I said I'm the best thing that could ever happen to you, and if you don't realize that by now, then you deserve to lose me!"

"Dani." It was hardly a breath, and when he reached out his arms, she was in them. He didn't know how it happened, he didn't know how any of it had happened. He could feel her shaking, and he held her tighter. The paper slipped from his fingers as he brought his hands up to caress her damp hair, and her fragrance, warm and lovely, drifted up to him, cinnamon and vanilla. Her shampoo. It had been her shampoo all along.

He could feel her breasts pressing into his chest, and her arms were tight and straining as they encircled his back. He felt a surge of strength and hot desire, a wash of weakness and disbelief, and he thought, *This is it. This is why I came home, this is all I ever wanted.* None of it made sense. He couldn't understand the miracle that had brought her to him, nor could he fully believe it was real, but it was, for the moment, enough that she was here, holding him, loving him. He parted his lips against her hair to better drink in her scent, her warmth, the dizzying, intoxicating *sureness* of her, and in a moment, he would turn his mouth to hers and then it would be too late for making sense, too late for second thoughts. So he released an unsteady breath and made his arms loosen a fraction. He looked down at her.

"Dani," he said hoarsely, "this is not a good idea."

And though it cost him more strength than he thought he possessed, he let his hands move down her arms, and he stepped back. "Just because I—I never should have written it down, and you never should have read it. I didn't want to mix up your life, I didn't want to cause trouble. Todd..."

She shook her head firmly, pressing her lips tightly together for a moment. "I gave Todd his ring back last night, before—before I even read your letter. I thought I had lost both of you, that's why I was so mad at you.... If I had known you felt the same way I did, I wouldn't have been so confused. I could have done the right thing a lot sooner. Oh, Bret, we've wasted so much time!"

"Years," he agreed softly. And he stood only inches away from her, drinking her in, aching for her, adrift in wonder and disbelief, yet paralyzed with uncertainty. Some things were too good to be true. Some things were never meant to be. He couldn't afford to make another mistake, not with Dani.

He made himself look away from her, half turning. He tried to take a breath, and found it more difficult than he anticipated. "Dani, this is...wow." He ran his fingers through his hair. "This isn't easy. We should talk."

"All right," she said quietly. She stood very still, watching him, and her gaze held him as tightly as her embrace had done. "I'll go first." She took a breath. "You always accused me of being afraid of change, but it's you, isn't it? You're the one who's afraid."

He started to shake his head in denial, but then heard himself saying, "Yes." He looked at her helplessly, wanting her and knowing he shouldn't, needing her and feeling the moment poised between his fingers, ready to grasp...seeing his whole life in her face, all that had ever had any meaning to him reflected in her eyes—and he was afraid, desperately afraid, of losing it.

"Things have already changed between us, Bret," she said softly. "They changed the first time you kissed me, and you know that, don't you? There's no going back. Why don't you kiss me now?"

"Dani, there's so much..." But he couldn't, at that moment, think of any of it. All the things that needed to be said, all the reasons this was wrong, all the cautions to be careful...they all seemed insignificant, faraway, and they diffused into meaningless puffs of smoke the moment he tried to grasp them. He wanted to be sensible, he wanted to do what was right for Dani, he wanted her to be able to count on him the way he had always counted on her.... But the only thing that seemed to matter was Dani, only a finger's length away, wanting him as much as he wanted her.

"Let it be easy," she whispered, and there was a hesitance in her eyes, almost a plea. "Things have always been so easy and right between us. I've wanted you for so long, and I hurt for you so much. Don't make it hurt now."

And it was easy. Her fingers touched his in a light gesture of reassurance, and his hand closed around hers. He turned her into his arms, meaning to comfort her, to hold her, to give them both a chance to think. But instead, his mouth was on hers, drinking in her startled breath of surprise, tasting her, drawing her in and letting himself drown in her, and it was easy and so right. She made him dizzy; she took away his power of thought. Her warmth baked through his skin, quickening his blood. He felt the frantic beating of her heart, almost lost in the thunder of his own, and the curve of her breast, just beneath his cupped hand, the length of her waist. He felt the straining of her small, tight muscles against his and the caress of her hand on the back of his neck, and the heat that filled his loins was heavy and painful, but that was right, too, inevitable and good.

Her hands were beneath his open jacket when the kiss ended, pulling it down, and that was the first time Bret realized he was still wearing his coat. He lowered his arms and let the jacket fall to the floor, and then he returned to her, caressing her face, the damp strands of her hair, the curve of her collarbone where it was exposed by the robe, and the shape of her shoulder. Her face was radiant, her lips swollen from his kisses, her breath as unsteady as his own. His eyes moved over hers, anxiously searching, then inevitably downward across her throat, the V of naked chest, the shape of her breasts.

He smiled, and said huskily, "You're not wearing anything under that robe, are you?"

She shook her head, and there might have been a flash of shyness in her eyes, or embarrassment. But it was gone in an instant and she held his gaze. "Are we going to make love, Bret?"

His heart lurched and pounded. Make love...with Dani. After all these years of thinking about it and pretending not to, of wanting and making himself not want... He traced the shape of her lips with an unsteady finger. "I don't see how we can help it."

She closed her eyes and swallowed. "Me, either," she whispered.

She lifted her hand to his, which was resting against the side of her face, and closed her fingers around it. She opened her eyes and made no attempt to hide what was written there: shyness, uncertainty, even a little fear, but most of all, wanting. She said, "Let's go upstairs."

Dani had climbed those stairs with Bret dozens of times before, but never had the walk seemed so long, so self-conscious, so fraught with tension. She wondered if they would have changed their minds before they arrived. She wondered if they were making a mistake. She wondered if she really wanted to do this, or if he did, and if, once they crossed this line, there would ever be a chance to go back to what they had been before...and she knew the answer to that was no, and she was afraid.

The bright morning sun streamed with unforgiving cheer over the bed, still made but rumpled with the imprint of Dani's restless night. Automatically, she moved to straighten the covers, but Bret caught her hand, smiling. After a moment, she returned the smile, recognizing her own silliness. He caressed her hair affectionately, a calming, soothing gesture.

"Feels funny, doesn't it?" she said.

He nodded. "I'm nervous."

Dani brought her hand uncertainly to her damp, tangled hair. "I look awful."

"You look like Dani."

She relaxed a little, entwining her fingers with his. "We never did have to pretend with each other, did we?"

His expression was sober. "Except about our feelings."

Tugging at his fingers, she crossed to the bed, and they sat down together. She was overwhelmed by the newness of it all, by expectation and excitement and uncertainty. Her stomach felt quivery and her muscles tight, and she knew Bret could feel her tension because he didn't rush her. She knew he wouldn't. He just sat there, holding her hand, watching her.

She tried to smile as she looked at him. "What have you got to be nervous about?"

A smile creased one corner of his mouth. "What all men have to be nervous about at a time like this, I guess. And more." His eyes sobered. "That you'll be disappointed. That we won't be good together. That we both expect too much and we're risking everything to find out. That we can never go back to what we were."

"I can't be disappointed," she said softly. "I've waited so long, wondered so long...."

A spark of surprise touched his eyes. "You've wondered about me?"

A soft laugh bubbled through her lips. "Don't tell me you didn't think girls had thoughts like that."

"Well, sure," he admitted. She could feel the tension leaving him in a low, easy ebb, just as it did her. "I knew you thought that way about other guys, but not about me. I never had a hint."

"How would you have felt if you'd known?"

He grinned. "I'm not sure I should answer that."

"Tell me," she insisted, bouncing on the bed a little as she rearranged her position, tucking one leg beneath her.

His grin became rueful. "Well, let's just say it wouldn't have done a whole lot for a teenage boy's self-control."

She was surprised. "Do you mean you used to think about me, too? About having sex with me?"

He nodded. "Remember all those times we used to practice making out in the backseat of my car? It's a good thing for both of us I had such strong character—and that I was so afraid of your father."

She laughed. "God, Bret, we were crazy. Both of us."

The smile in his eyes grew thoughtful. "Funny, I never thought about it before. I guess you taught me everything I know about the opposite sex, without even meaning to."

"You taught me, too," she agreed softly. "A lot of things."

He looked at her soberly. "It wasn't just as a kid, either. Over the years... I've thought about making love to you a lot. It always made me feel kind of strange."

"Like now," she agreed.

He dropped his gaze, and his fingers traced the undercurve of her knee where it was exposed by the parting of her robe. Her skin prickled with the touch; her heart beat a little faster.

"I know everything about you," he said softly, "except this. I don't know what you like, how to make it good for you, how to even begin. I feel like I'm with a stranger...or like this is the first time I've ever made love."

Dani's throat tightened a little. "I don't know how to please you, either."

He looked up at her and smiled, his hand resting on her knee. "We could always talk dirty to each other for a little while."

"We could," she agreed slowly, and there was a touch of wonder in her voice. "We really could. And it wouldn't embarrass us, would it?"

The deepening of understanding in his eyes reflected her own, and with the simple dawning of truth, the last residue of awkwardness between them slipped away. "No," he said simply. "We're too close to be embarrassed about anything."

"But I'm still shy," she admitted.

"Why?"

"Because you've never seen me naked before."

His eyes twinkled. "Wrong. We took baths together until we were six, remember?"

"I've changed a little since then."

"You're forgetting the hole the boys drilled in the wall of the girls' locker room in high school."

"You didn't!" She struck out at him playfully, and he caught her arms, laughing, overbalancing her until she fell backward on the bed and he was poised above her, one leg thrown lightly over both of hers, his face only inches from hers.

Her breath caught, and then was released in a shallow flutter, fanning across his face. His eyes were a mixture of darks and lights, intense and penetrating, yet welcoming, wonderfully familiar. He said softly, "How do you feel now?"

"Kind of... hot and quivery inside," she replied breathlessly. "Nervous, but not afraid. Happy." So happy.

He dropped a slow, gentle kiss on her forehead. "I think I know where to start now."

He stood up and began to remove his clothes.

Dani turned onto her side, pillowing her cheek with her hand, and watched as he pulled off his boots and socks, then drew his sweatshirt over his head in a single, fluid motion and discarded it on the floor. His hands dropped to the snap of his jeans, then hesitated. He came over to the bed and sat beside her.

"Change your mind?" Dani teased, but her voice was a little husky because, although she was sure she had seen his naked chest before as an adult, possibly even been this close to it, his nearness made her pulses skip and her throat go dry.

The crinkles at the corners of his eyes deepened, and he wound a strand of her hair around his index finger, releasing it into a damp corkscrew. "You never heard of the allure of the wrapped package?"

"I kind of like what's unwrapped," she said. But he was right. The excitement of having him sit beside her shirtless was more enticing than had he taken her in a naked embrace, because what was happening between them deserved to be savored moment by moment, because there was the promise of more and because so much time had been lost to them now that nothing could be rushed; every second was precious.

She had always known Bret was an attractive man, but she had never known it in such a personal way before. His chest was lean and tanned, lightly sprinkled with golden hair. The pectoral muscles were firm, centered by flat, brown nipples that were slightly puckered in the room temperature. She could kiss his chest if she wanted to. She could touch him. And she did want to.

She lifted her hand, trailing her fingers down the sharp divide of his collarbone, spreading her palm over the expanse of one pectoral muscle, then sliding it down over his ribs and his waist, until her fingers met the impediment of his jeans. His pleasure at her touch was reflected in his eyes, and he smiled, tucking his fingers under her chin. "Something else I don't know about you," he said.

"What?"

"Whether you like to do the unwrapping your-self."

A flush went through her, excited and weakening, and her heart beat harder with surprise for the inti-macy of the suggestion—the one thing she had never imagined herself doing, undressing Bret. Her fingers moved along the circle of his waistband, and she whispered, "Yes. I think I do."

"So do I." He leaned forward and tugged at the sash of her robe.

He parted the material, and she caught her breath as his eyes moved over her, filled with slow, gentle lights of pleasure. And following his eyes were his hands, pushing the sleeves of the robe off her arms, caressing her arms, cupping her heavy breasts in his hands, moving down over her stomach and outlining the shape of her hips, upward again along the length of her thighs. She was suspended in the wonder of his touch, tingling with new sparks of surprise in every caress; she could hardly breathe.

And then he lifted his eyes to hers again, smiling. "Not fair, Dani," he murmured huskily. "I thought you were going to do some unwrapping."

Her throat felt swollen, her heart beating hard as she moved her fingers to the snap of his jeans. The zipper was stubborn, and she could feel his heat and hardness against her fingers. She tugged the zipper downward and he stood up, allowing her to pull his jeans and his briefs over his hips. He stepped out of the garments and came back to her, resting his weight on one knee on the bed beside her. She looked upon the part of him that she had never known before, strong in his arousal, and she wanted to touch him. She felt the catch of his breath as she reached out her hand, brushing his inner thigh with her fingertips, encircling the strong, hard length of him with her hand.

He smothered a groan and stretched out beside her, drawing her into his arms. Their mouths met in a single surge of hunger and need, a wash of heat, a perfect blending. With an eager, almost desperate greed, Dani's hands moved over him, delighting in his broad angles and lean lines, the intimate parts of him, the strong and the soft. Bret, just as he had always been; hers, just as he had always been.

He drew her onto her side, encircling her with one leg, his hand sweeping down her back and cupping her buttocks, pressing her close. "Dani," he murmured against her neck, "look how well we fit together."

"Yes," she whispered, dizzy with wonder, and then she lost her breath as he lowered his head, placing a deep kiss upon her breast, drawing her nipple into his mouth, encircling it with his tongue. His hand slipped between her thighs, and her heart shattered in her chest as his fingertips caressed the sensitive inner flesh of her legs, then moved upward, his palm pressing firmly against the swollen, aching center of her. The sensation was so intense that a cry caught in her throat, and her fingernails dug into his shoulder.

"I know," he whispered, his lips brushing across her face. "I know..." He shifted above her; her legs opened to receive him, and in the space of one long, suspended heartbeat, he filled her.

He caught her face between his hands, and she opened her eyes to a delirium of joy: the beauty of his face poised above her, flushed and damp, his eyes a blaze of lights and darks, of tenderness and wonder; the fullness that was him inside her, a part of her, complete. Never had she known such completeness, because it was Bret, and it was so right.

She moved her hands over his back, she threaded her fingers into his hair. He kissed her face, his tongue lightly tasting her lips, and he began to move inside her, gentle-stroking caresses that caused her to gasp out loud with pleasure, with wonder, with the power of the sensations he built within her. She rose to meet him, and their rhythms became more urgent, a spiral of need and wanting that went beyond physical union. And as the power of fulfillment burst upon them, they touched in that moment the parts of each other they had never known before, each a part of the other; they knew and they held and they treasured what had been missing for all their lives. It was right. It was perfect.

Sunshine danced over their perspiration-slickened bodies, warmer than summertime as it was magnified through the high window. They lay on their backs close together, Dani's ankle curved over one of his. Bret's arm rested across her stomach. Sunbeams broke in slow, colorful explosions behind Dani's closed eyes in rhythm with the gradually slowing thunder of her heart. She could hear Bret's breathing; she could feel the glow of his body heat spreading over her and through her, still a part of her. She opened her eyes, experiencing a renewed thrill at seeing him naked beside her, at discovering his eyes adoring her even before she looked at him.

She threaded her fingers through his, turning her face on the pillow so that it was only inches away from his. "So what do you think?" she said softly. "Are we good together?"

He released a long, low breath and moved his arm to encircle her waist, drawing her close. "Ah, Dani, I could spend the rest of my life making love to you."

And they would, Dani thought. A little shiver of wonder went through her as she tightened her arms around him. They had the rest of their lives to do just that.

She lay back against the pillow, smiling with simple, silly joy. "Are you surprised?" she questioned. "Everything we do together is good."

"Yeah," he admitted slowly. His own smile was drowsy and love dazed. "I am surprised. It seems too good to be true, somehow. More than I deserve."

"Oh, Bret." She caressed his face, loving him so intensely that she had to close her eyes for a moment, lest the emotion spill over into tears. "I think...I know what you mean."

They lay together in silence for a while, locked in wonder and the simple, quiet pleasure of being together. Dani stretched out her hand, caressing his thigh. She loved the feel of that strong length of musculature, the light furring of hair, the heated crevice where his leg joined his pelvis, the stirring of his arousal against her fingertips. She felt his slow, indrawn breath, and then, reluctantly, he reached down and caught her hand.

"Honey, don't," he said huskily. "We can't stay here all day."

Her eyes sparkled as she playfully struggled to free her fingers. "Why not?"

"Because," he replied, determinedly tightening his hold and bringing her fingers to his lips. "It's the middle of the morning and I've got to get out of here. I'm supposed to be shoveling your walk, and you're supposed to be doing one of your busy Christmas elf things. And if we stay here much longer, your parents are going to start to wonder."

"Still afraid of my father?" she teased.

"You better believe it." Bret started to sit up, but she trapped him with one leg thrown across his abdomen. Delight sparked in his eyes even as he caught her shoulders, gently but firmly turning her back to her own pillow, holding her with a light pressure of his hands. "You are a witch," he said. "Something else I didn't know about you."

The playfulness in his eyes faded into gentle reluctance as he added, "But I've got to get serious with you for a minute, okay?"

Dani's hand, which had been playing with his hair, came to rest against the side of his face. She met his eyes a little uncertainly, but not afraid. She nodded.

"Dani," he said, "this isn't going to be easy for a lot of reasons. And one of them is your parents. I wouldn't hurt them or have them think badly of me for anything in the world. They still think you're— Well, you're with Todd. And until you can get things straightened out, we're going to have to be discreet."

Dani nodded, understanding. "So you're going to go shovel the walk, and I'm going to get dressed and go help Mom bake fruitcakes, is that it?"

She could see in his eyes that he found the idea just as bizarre, just as impossible as she did. But he said, "I think it's best."

She sat up, and Bret watched as she reached for the telephone, punching out a few digits. In a moment, she spoke into the receiver. "Hello, Mom? I broke up with Todd last night and now I'm sleeping with Bret. Is that okay?"

She moved the mouthpiece away a little and told Bret, "She says it's okay."

It was all she could do to keep from shouting with laughter at the look of stunned horror on his face, and the amusement in her eyes must have given her away. For just then, he noticed her finger remained on the disconnect button. He snatched the receiver from her, pushing her down on the bed, covering her with his body. "You *are* a witch!" he declared, his eyes dancing with laughter. "And I love you more than I ever loved anyone in my life."

"Oh, Bret." She cupped his face, adoring it, adoring him. "Why did it take you so long to tell me? Why did you have to keep it a secret?"

His eyes sobered a little. "Maybe," he answered, "for the same reason you kept it a secret ten years ago."

She looked confused. "What?"

"You wrote it down," he reminded her. "The night before I got married. That's why I came home, Dani. I finally got your letter."

"My letter?" Bewilderment and uncertainty tangled within her. "But... but I threw it away. I'm sure I did...."

"Just like I threw mine away."

"All those years ago..." She shook her head against the pillow, suffused with confusion and disbelief. "But that's not possible. Bret, you must be mistaken. There's no way..."

He smiled, slipping one hand beneath her, stroking her hip. "Do you know what I think we've got here?" he said.

The bewilderment left her, and she hardly heard the words, concentrated as she was on the caressing strokes of his hand, moving now around and upward, urging her thighs apart, teasing and caressing.

"What?" she whispered.

"A miracle," he answered.

And as she felt him move against her, sliding slowly inside, she wrapped her arms around him, and she thought with wonderment, *Yes. A miracle...*

Chapter Twelve

When Bret awoke the next morning, a hazy early sunlight was filtering through the loft window and Dani
was sleeping in his arms. He hadn't really spent the
entire previous day and night in her bed, though it felt
like it. The time when he had been away from her was
so blurred and indistinct in memory that it seemed not
to have existed at all, and in a way, he supposed it
hadn't. Nothing was real to him except the time he had
spent with her.

Sometime after lunch, he had gotten around to
shoveling the walk, and Dani had come outside and
thrown snowballs at him. When Harold pulled up in
his truck and asked Bret if he wanted to ride into town
with him, Bret thought it would be politic to accept.
When the two men returned, Dani was in the kitchen
with her mother, the house smelled of cinnamon and
nutmeg, and Dani asked Bret casually if he would like
to come over and help her make spaghetti for dinner.
He went.

She had told her mother about Todd, but Bret had
not gotten around to asking what else she had said.
Not that it mattered, now. His hosts would have had

to have been blind not to realize he hadn't come home last night, and not to guess where he had been.

He hadn't intended to spend the night. He must have started to leave four or five times, only to be stopped by one last kiss, one more embrace or some tart remark from Dani that would make him laugh or remind him of a story or set off a shared reminiscence. For they had not spent all of their time making love. In fact, some of the best hours had been spent simply holding each other, talking quietly or not talking at all, feeling good and warm and secure, making up for all the time that had gone before.

On Dani's bedside table sat the withered cactus. She had plucked it out of a trash can yesterday and had refused to tell him why. It had made him smile then, and it made him smile now, as he looked at it. Only today the smile was a little sad.

It was amazing. Yesterday, in the heady euphoria of physical love, of runaway emotions, of simple, obsessive joy, the problems that confronted them had seemed to simply disappear. He couldn't think beyond the moment, time did not exist beyond the next embrace, and it simply had not occurred to him that there was any life outside the sparkle of Dani's smile, the warmth of her arms. And maybe that was why he had spent the night, despite his better judgment. Because he knew, on some deep inner level, how precious the moments were and that daylight would inevitably come.

She was so beautiful, cuddled up in the curve of his arm, her hair tousled and her cheeks flushed with sleep. It was so easy to imagine a thousand mornings like this, a hundred thousand....

He grasped her shoulder and shook her gently. "Hey," he said softly. "Wake up."

She was smiling even before she opened her eyes. He smiled back, adoring her.

"We are in big trouble, kid," he said. "It's morning."

"I know." She stretched up her arms, encircling his neck, looking up at him with drowsy, love-sated eyes. "It was wonderful sleeping with you, Bret. Not just making love, but sleeping together."

"I know." He drew her close, bringing his face to her hair, inhaling deeply. She smelled incredible. "Like we've been doing it for years. Like it always should have been."

She bent her head back, looking at him with a slightly studious expression.

"Can I ask you something?"

"What?"

"Do you always sleep in the nude?"

His eyes picked up a spark of delight that came from nothing more than looking at her. "Not always. Sometimes I wear my shorts."

"Don't you get cold?"

He kissed her lightly on the nose. "Not in California."

And there it was, the moment they had both in their secret ways been dreading, the subject they had been trying to avoid. He saw the shadow touch her eyes even as it chilled his soul, and she started to speak.

He sat up abruptly. "Wait," he said, perhaps a bit too cheerfully. "I almost forgot. I have a Christmas present for you. I was going to give it to you yesterday, before I—" *Before he left town.* He didn't have to say the words; they rang implicitly in the air.

He reached over the side of the bed and brought up his pants, digging in the pocket for a gift-wrapped box. Dani smiled a little hesitantly as she took it. "The last time I got an early Christmas present, it made me cry. For about eight hours."

He ruffled her hair gently. "This one won't make you cry, I promise. At least, not for eight hours."

She looked up at him, suddenly stricken by a superstitious fear. "Do I have to open it now? Can't it wait for Christmas?"

He seemed to understand and smiled in quick reassurance. "Sure it can. Put it under the tree, and if you can keep your hands off it till Christmas morning, it's yours."

He swung his legs over the side of the bed and began to pull on his pants. "If you'll tell me where you keep the makings, I'll go down and do the coffee."

Dani tried to keep the anxiety out of her voice as she said, "It's just that giving it to me now makes me think that . . . well, that you might not be here for Christmas."

She saw the long muscles of his back tense, and his silence stabbed at her heart, taking her breath away. "Bret?"

He turned around. "I'll be here for Christmas," he assured her quickly, but the words were not enough. There was a mixture of reluctance and dread in his eyes as he searched hers, and the tension did not leave his shoulders.

"I'll probably have to go home for a little while," he went on carefully, "to take care of the final paperwork on the sale. And I need to check in with the office. But I'll be back."

She spoke hesitantly, not wanting to, knowing she shouldn't. "To stay?"

He looked away and didn't answer.

Dani reached for her robe and pushed her arms into the sleeves, feeling suddenly numb and cold. Bret stood up and pulled on his sweatshirt. Dani swung the covers aside and bent to put on her slippers, trying to pretend as though everything was normal, as though the weight of the whole world wasn't suddenly pressing her down... but she couldn't.

Her voice was small and a little shaky as she said, "Oh, Bret, what's going to happen to us?"

He drew in a breath and turned. His expression was cautious, not quite hopeful, and his eyes were busy searching her face, anticipating her every thought and reflecting it back to her. "I've been thinking. When the electronics plant opens, I can make a bid for the security contract. That doesn't mean I'll get it, but even if I don't, if there's one thing I do know, it's electronics. I can get a job."

The relief that went through Dani came in waves, uncertain and hopeful. He didn't want to leave her. They could work it out. There was a chance....

But he wasn't finished. "Honey, we've got to be realistic. A thousand things could go wrong. At best, it'll be a year or two before the plant is even open, and in the meantime, I have a business to run. I can't afford to keep two households. You'll have to come back with me for a while."

Of course. It was a simple solution, the only possible solution. She couldn't let him go, not after all the wasted years; he couldn't stay here, not without a job. But... "California?" she managed, in a tight, uncertain voice. "You want me to go with you to California?"

A flash of impatience crossed his eyes. "It's not Jupiter, for God's sake. They've got schools there, hundreds of them. You can get a job anywhere. And it'll only be for a little while—"

"Or maybe not," she said softly.

For reality, as clear and certain as it had ever been, spread itself before her. This was not a daydream, and even miracles like the one she had found with Bret were not always perfect. He was talking about an entirely new way of life, leaving behind the only home she had ever known, her family, her friends, the children she loved and the people she had grown up with. Herself. She would be leaving behind *herself*.

And once there, anything could happen. Bret had a business, roots, an entirely separate life on the West Coast, and it would be hard to give it up. And even if they did come home in a few years... there would be no home to come back to. Everything would be different.

She felt ill inside, disoriented and unsure. It shouldn't be this way. Things between them had always been so easy; why couldn't this be, too? But she couldn't help it. She was afraid.

Dani turned away, hugging her elbows, but not before she saw an expression of the most exquisite sadness come over Bret's face. "Now I remember," he said quietly.

"What?" Her voice sounded tinny and dull.

"The fight we had just before I went away to college. I wanted you to come with me, remember? With all your talent, you could have made it in Hollywood, you could have at least given it a try...."

She shook her head fiercely. "That's not what I wanted to do. I never wanted—"

"To take a chance," he finished for her flatly. "You let your whole life pass you by because you were afraid to find out what was on the other side of the mountain."

"That's not true!" she cried, turning to him. "You never understood that! I knew what I wanted, Bret, and it wasn't in California. *You're* the one who didn't know, who had to keep searching—"

"All those years," he said bitterly. "All those years wasted because you wouldn't come with me. I loved you then, Dani, just as much as I love you now, I just didn't know how to say the words. And now it's happening all over again."

"It doesn't have to!" she insisted desperately. "Don't you see Bret, the life I have here is good. It could be good for you, too, you know it could, and for our children! You don't have to walk away from it all. You don't have to destroy it. Why can't you just be happy? Why can't you let *us* be happy?"

But the look on his face was one of utter defeat and deepest regret, and he did not have to put his feelings into words. He sat on the bed and began to pull on his boots. "It was never a matter of life-styles," he said tiredly. "Or even values. I guess I was just hoping that this time, maybe you'd trust me enough to take a chance on me."

He stood up, his expression bleak and weary. "I'm sorry, Dani. I don't have any other solution."

He went down the stairs and out the door.

Dani pressed her lips together tightly, gripping her elbows to stop the trembling, refusing to give into despair, refusing to accept this as the end. They had come so far; they had found so much. It wasn't fair. How could he give up now?

How could she?

There had to be an answer. There just *had* to be.

Her eyes fell on the small wrapped package on the bed, and she picked it up. She knew she shouldn't open it. She knew it would make her cry.

She pushed aside the wrapping paper and opened the box. Slowly, she drew out the charm bracelet with its single silver bell and held it up to the light from the window. On the side of the bell, much like another bell from long ago, was an engraving: BU + DG.

She had been right. It made her cry.

BRET LET HIMSELF INTO the house through the enclosed back porch, stripping off his muddy boots and adding them to the stack by the door, angrily discarding his coat. He started toward the kitchen, from which the bright warmth of a light was already glowing, but he couldn't make himself go in. His lips tightened as he braced his hands against the door frame, and he wanted to beat his head against the wall, driving out the anger, the pain, the confusion. Instead, he brought his forehead slowly to rest against the cool wood, breathing deeply, trying to think clearly.

He had known this was going to happen; he had expected it. He had expected it so much he had *made* it happen, and he felt like a fool. All these years of loving Dani without even knowing it, of needing her, depending on her... was he going to throw it all away now because of one stupid argument about where they were going to *live?*

It was more than that, of course. He had asked her to share his life, and she had cut him to the core with her hesitance, that look of shock and reluctance in her eyes. She loved him, but he wasn't worth changing for. But he had hurt her, as well, by refusing to share her life, by insisting, in fact, on taking away everything she had built her life around. They had both opened wounds from the past that should have long since healed, but neither one was able to let go.

He kept telling himself that it was impossible to stay here with her, as much as he wanted to, and in a practical way, it was. But now he was forced to admit that the only reason he had left in the first place was fear: fear of losing himself in this place, of settling for small dreams and simple victories, of never taking the chance on finding out what he could be. But he had found out. He had followed the dream, he had climbed the mountain, and now he had come home. And he was too stupid to realize that he was still fighting a battle that had been won a long time ago.

He straightened up slowly, a weight dropping from his shoulders, the cobwebs melting away from his mind. He *had* been stupid. Both of them had. Each of them had been deliberately, although not entirely consciously, reenacting the past, and the past didn't matter anymore. They had found what they wanted. Now they simply had to decide whether they were strong enough to accept it.

He opened the kitchen door and went inside.

The room was bathed in good, clean, kitchen light and smelled of perking coffee and cinnamon rolls. Miss Annie, in a bright, flowered robe, turned from the stove and smiled at him, just as though it were the most natural thing in the world that he should come sneaking in the back door at six o'clock in the morning after an all-night tryst with her daughter.

"Good morning, Bret. Coffee's almost ready."

The warmth of home washed over him, a familiar, loving face, redolent with memories and continuity and all that was solid, dependable and good about life. Was he really going to sweep all this aside? How could he ask Dani to turn her back on them? How could he ask it of himself?

He stood there for a moment, feeling dazed and a little overwhelmed, but strengthened inside with a growing certainty. Then he murmured, "Umm, excuse me, Miss Annie. I've got to make a phone call."

He found his address book and searched through the pages for Craig Notion's home number. He paused for only a minute with his hand on the receiver, wondering if it could possibly be he, Bret Underwood, who was about to blow the deal of a lifetime, wondering if he could possibly be considering snatching away a whole town's future for the sake of one woman's happiness . . . and then he punched out the numbers.

Craig's voice, heavy with sleep, answered on the third ring.

"Are you crazy?" he demanded groggily when Bret identified himself. "Do you have any idea what time it is here?"

"I wanted to get you before you left for the office."

"Well, you sure as hell did that."

"Listen, Craig. I want you to do something for me." He took a breath. "Cancel the Inushu deal. I've decided not to sell."

There was a pause, and Bret braced himself for the storm of accusations, protests and invectives. But when Craig's voice came back, it was laced with sarcasm and sounded slightly bored. "Yeah, well, smart boy. For this you wake me up before sunrise?"

Bret frowned at the receiver, uncertain he had heard correctly. "You're not mad?"

"I might be one of the fastest wheeler-dealers in Southern California, my boy, but even I don't get my clients in bed with companies that are getting ready to go bankrupt."

"What?"

"What's the matter, you don't read the financial pages anymore? Or don't you get newspapers out in the sticks? It was all over the *Wall Street Journal* yesterday—and just in damn time, too. Looks like they were trying to keep their real financial picture secret until they could fatten up their assets a little, hoping for a takeover. Yours wasn't the only deal they were trying to rush through before the end of the year.''

Bret sat back in his chair, the strength suddenly leaving his muscles. "Do you mean—if I had made the sale, there never would have been any electronics plant?" No new jobs, new housing, roads, county revenues....

"Hardly. The whole company would probably have fallen victim to some corporate raider, been parceled off...you know how these things go. You might've gotten your money, and you might not have, but it would've been years, and maybe ten cents on the dollar. As for the property, who knows? Not that it would've mattered by that time."

"No," Bret murmured, stunned. "Not that it would've mattered."

"I'm surprised you don't know more about this than I do. Seems I remember a sidebar that said the whole investigation was stirred up by a newspaperman down your way. Can you beat that? The best financial journalists in the whole country scooped by some hick reporter who didn't want an electronics plant built in his backyard."

"Todd." But it was hardly more than a whisper, and Craig didn't hear.

"Well, I'm sorry it worked out this way." Craig's voice was heavy. "Good thing I didn't spend that commission. Merry Christmas, as they say."

"Yeah." Bret's lips began to twitch with the beginnings of a slow, disbelieving grin. "Merry Christmas."

The grin spread along with the wonder, and by the time he hung up the phone, Bret was laughing, softly, all to himself alone in the room.

DANI SPLASHED WATER ON her face, shook back her hair and squared her shoulders determinedly. "Dani Griffin," she told the woman in the mirror, "you are an idiot."

She took the stairs two at a time, pulling on her coat as she left the house, and plodded through the snow across the drive.

"Mom," she demanded breathlessly as she burst into the kitchen, "where's Bret?"

Her mother complacently set another place at the table. "He went for a walk. He didn't say where."

"That's okay." Dani turned quickly for the door. "I think I know."

"Dani." Her mother looked up, the faintest trace of concern shadowing her brow. "Wait a minute. There's something you should know."

DANI TOOK THE FAMILIAR path through the woods, pushing aside ice-stiffened branches, following the footprints in the snow. The footprints ended at the edge of the woods, and there Bret stood, his hands shoved into his pockets, gazing out over the pine-studded fields toward the house beyond. Dani hesitated for a moment, infused with wonder and adoration for the figure he made, standing alone in the snow. Then she made her way over to him.

He must have heard her footsteps, but he did not turn. They stood together in silence for a while, sharing the view. Then Dani said, "Remember in second grade when Len Bueler and his buddies tried to ambush you after school?"

A small smile of reminiscence touched Bret's lips. "You came out swinging with your lunchbox. Len had to have stitches."

"And in eighth grade, when we both auditioned for first chair in the school orchestra?"

"You played badly so that I would get it."

"And then you played so badly, neither one of us got it."

His smile deepened.

Dani touched his arm, making him look at her. "If I stood by you all those times," she said softly, "what makes you think I won't stand by you in this?"

Bret's expression softened in wordless love and gratitude, and he slipped one arm around her waist, drawing her close. Dani leaned her head against his shoulder, filled with the strength of his nearness, the wonder of loving him. For a time, she couldn't speak.

Then she said quietly, "Mom told me about the land deal."

Bret's voice was heavy. "You and Todd were right all along."

"You called off the sale before you even knew about the bankruptcy."

"Still, it was a close call. If it hadn't been for Todd..."

"Another Christmas miracle," she said, coaxing a smile from Bret.

But his eyes were a little sad. "We've about used up our share, haven't we?" He shook his head a little.

"The funny thing is, I kept telling myself I was doing it for you, for the town—even for Todd—despite what you all wanted. I thought progress was the only way. But now I see there are some things worth preserving. The world moves so fast, we're very, very lucky if we can hold on to the good things. Only now...I just don't know how."

Dani squeezed his arm bracingly. "So we go to California. I'm about due for a change. All this snow and slush is starting to get on my nerves."

He turned to her, smoothing back her hair with a gloved hand. Tenderness and wonder gentled his eyes. "You'd do that?"

"You'd do the same for me," she told him simply. "As a matter of fact, you just did."

He drew her into a slow, loving embrace. "Ah, Dani," he murmured into her hair. "You'd hate it in California. I hate it there. I just wish—"

"Ssh..." She lifted her hand to touch his face. "We don't have to decide right now. There's plenty of time to make plans. After Christmas. It can wait till after Christmas."

Their lips met in a long, deep kiss that spread its glow like radiant embers, full of promise, strong in its certainty. Yes, they had had their share of miracles. They didn't need any more.

When the kiss was over, they stood together, Dani's head against Bret's shoulder, their arms around each other's waists. They had no need for words, but simply stood in warmth and silence, watching the sun rise.

The scrubby, barren fields no longer looked ugly to Bret. The rising sun glinted off the snow-frosted pine trees, making them dance with a hundred Christmas lights. In fact, everything around him, as far as he could see, was dressed up like a Christmas-tree lot, a winter fantasy land. And slowly, tenuously, an incredible idea began to stir within him.

He could feel a slight reciprocal tension in Dani's body, and her voice was small with cautious excitement. "Do you remember," she ventured, "your dad used to say if there was a profit in rocks and pine trees . . ."

"Not only pines," he heard himself murmuring, "but spruce and fir . . ."

She lifted her eyes to him, and they reflected the shock and the wonder that was in his own. It was so simple. So absurdly simple.

"I don't know anything about tree farming," he said, but his hands gripped her arms as excitement began to buzz through his head—plans to be made, possibilities to be explored.

"George Skinner does!" she declared.

"If he would stay on and manage it for me—"

"And not just trees, but greenhouses! A nursery—"

"It doesn't have to stop here. The other farmers in the county have hundreds of acres going fallow—"

"A co-op!" she cried. "Evergreens will grow anywhere! We could ship all over the country!"

They were in each other's arms, laughing, hugging, holding on tight. He seized her shoulders, trying to think carefully, trying to be practical, but unable to keep the excitement from blazing in his eyes. "I could sell the business," he said, "and maybe make enough to get us through the lean years. But, honey, it's a hell of a chance—''

"And about time we took one," she replied.

She went into his arms again, and he buried his face in her hair, breathing deeply, cherishing the moment. "Sometimes," he murmured, "I guess we have to make our own miracles."

And Dani smiled, holding him. "Most of the time," she said.

ON THE NIGHT TABLE in Dani's loft, a single cactus blossom slowly unfurled beneath the husk of a long dormancy, and Christmas had arrived.

HARLEQUIN
AMERICAN ROMANCE
brings you

Season's Greetings

When a magical, red-cheeked, white-bearded postman delivers long-lost letters, the lives of four unsuspecting couples will change forever.

Experience all the magic of Christmas with these special books.

Don't miss: #418 CHRISTMAS IN TOYLAND
by Julie Kistler
#419 AN ANGEL IN TIME
by Stella Cameron
#420 FOR AULD LANG SYNE
by Pamela Browning

Christmas—the season when wishes *do* come true....

Take 4 bestselling love stories FREE

Plus get a FREE surprise gift!

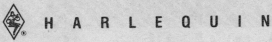

H A R L E Q U I N

A Calendar of Romance

Be a part of American Romance's year-long celebration of love and the holidays of 1992. Experience all the passion of falling in love during the excitement of each month's holiday. Some of your favorite authors will help you celebrate those special times of the year, like the revelry of New Year's Eve, the romance of Valentine's Day, the magic of St. Patrick's Day.

Start counting down to the new year with

#421 HAPPY NEW YEAR, DARLING
by Margaret St. George

Read all the books in *A Calendar of Romance*, coming to you one each month, all year, from Harlequin American Romance.

American Romance®

COR1